122

LOGAN

BROTHERHOOD PROTECTORS WORLD

REGAN BLACK

Twisted Page Press LLC

BROTHERHOOD PROTECTORS

ORIGINAL SERIES BY ELLE JAMES

Brotherhood Protectors Series

Montana SEAL (#1)

Bride Protector SEAL (#2)

Montana D-Force (#3)

Cowboy D-Force (#4)

Montana Ranger (#5)

Montana Dog Soldier (#6)

Montana SEAL Daddy (#7)

Montana Ranger's Wedding Vow (#8)

Montana SEAL Undercover Daddy (#9)

Cape Cod SEAL Rescue (#10)

Montana SEAL Friendly Fire (#11)

Montana SEAL's Mail-Order Bride (#12)

SEAL Justice (#13)

Ranger Creed (#14)

Delta Force Rescue (#15)

Montana Rescue (Sleeper SEAL)

Hot SEAL Salty Dog (SEALs in Paradise)

Hot SEAL Hawaiian Nights (SEALs in Paradise)

Hot SEAL Bachelor Party (SEALs in Paradise)

Brotherhood Protectors World
Guardian Agency: Logan
By Regan Black

~

As always, with special thanks to Elle James for inviting
me into her world of
Brotherhood Protectors.
And for my readers, your love for these Guardian Agency
heroes
makes my world brighter every day.

~

ABOUT GUARDIAN AGENCY: LOGAN
When hope is lost, truth is blurred, and your life is on the
line, it's time to call
the Guardian Agency...

The invisible wounds are the hardest to heal...
Months ago, Allison Weaver's boyfriend turned violent
after one of his investments tanked. She left him
immediately, but the incident shattered her confidence.
Now he's harassing her with threats and accusations that
her research into an historical site in Charleston, South
Carolina has derailed his newest business deal.

Can her best friend teach her to trust-and possibly love-
again?
Logan Harris is home for good and eager to reconnect
with his best friend, Allison, the one person he truly
missed during his career as a Marine. But on their first
night out as friends, he catches her ex hassling her.

Protecting Allison is second nature and sticking close
while he sorts out the danger reveals an unprecedented
attraction sparking between them. But when her relentless
ex gets more aggressive, Logan must call in additional
resources in order to keep her safe and preserve any hope
of a future together.

Visit ReganBlack.com for a full list of books, excerpts and
upcoming release dates.

For early access to new releases, exclusive prizes, and much more,
subscribe to Regan's monthly newsletter.

CHAPTER 1

As the last student walked out of his classroom, Logan Harris stood and stretched his arms overhead, arching his back until he heard a series of pops along his spine. His body was still learning how to be a civilian. Though he kept up his workouts, he missed the hard demands of active duty.

Of all the things the Marine Corps had asked of him, teaching a class on the history of the Corps at the Citadel in Charleston, South Carolina was as clean, straightforward, and soft as a mission could get. Not easy, per se, but a far cry from a typical deployment or training exercise. He was actually enjoying himself, the students, and pace of the summer programming.

With only two weeks under his belt as an interim

professor—still shocked him to hear that title in conjunction with his name—the faculty had extended an offer to bring him on full-time in the fall. The full time offer came with distinct advantages of great pay and plenty of breaks with the school year calendar. Still, it put an itch between his shoulder blades thinking about it. He wasn't ready for a career indoors behind a desk. Although he didn't need the work, he wasn't at liberty to discuss his recently signed agreement with an extremely private security company.

The Guardian Agency didn't publicize their services, operating solely on word of mouth and personal recommendations. Which said a lot for their success rate considering their central office was on Michigan Avenue in Chicago and they were actively hiring. Work as a bodyguard felt like the smart fit for his top skills and his plans to figure out life as a civilian. And his intention to plant roots in this area hadn't fazed his agency contact, Patrick Gamble. In fact, they seemed pleased to add Logan to their roster in this region.

Though he'd been born and raised in a town not far from Charleston, his trips home were few after completing his initial training at Parris Island. So far, it felt good to be back. Even the steep summer humidity felt familiar and comforting. He needed the familiar right now.

He stretched again. His stiff back was proof enough he needed more movement than standing during fifty minute lectures in an air-conditioned classroom. Shutting down his laptop, he tucked it into his messenger bag and plucked the keys to the school-provided rental house from the desk drawer. He could drop everything at the house and go for a walk. He was looking forward to exploring the city some more now that his day was over.

The city had changed and grown in his absence. Some of his favorite haunts had changed hands and become new businesses, but plenty of the places he loved were still there, barely altered.

He checked his watch as he locked the classroom door. If he timed it right, maybe he'd run into Allison Weaver. Discovering his best friend from high school was also on the summer faculty had been an amazing bonus. He hadn't laid eyes on Allison since the day before their graduation. He'd skipped the pomp and circumstance of the event itself and the parties that followed, too eager to get on with the rest of his life as a Marine.

If his temporary role as an instructor got back to any of his old teachers they wouldn't believe it.

Allison was a natural fit. She'd been a top student and eventually became a history professor at the College of Charleston. Logan hadn't applied himself to any particular class or goal until the Corps.

Logan couldn't think of two stranger paths to cross here and now. In the past twelve years they hadn't done more than exchange Christmas cards. Well, Allison sent cards to him and, in the years he'd been stateside, he sent one back. He never questioned how she'd found his address, she'd always been resourceful. It meant the world to him that she cared enough to make the effort.

Since his return, she was an invaluable touchstone after what had felt like months of floundering and not fitting in anywhere. More importantly, she'd made it clear she was willing—possibly even eager—to rekindle their friendship. A gift he would *not* take for granted.

It had been more than a decade since he'd had a true friend outside of the Marines. Everyone else from his past had tumbled out of contact, people he remembered fondly, but were no longer part of his life. Friends he now missed. Leaving the Corps was the right decision. He just hadn't expected it to take so much time to feel like himself again as a civilian.

He paused at a window in the long hallway, appreciating the unique view of Charleston. After traveling the world, seeing amazing sights and dreadful ugliness, the peninsula smoothed out the frayed edges of his soul.

"Penny for your thoughts."

He swiveled around to find Allison watching him, a smile on her pretty face. "Hey."

The early afternoon light pouring through the big windows turned the sun-streaked highlights in her brown hair to shimmering gold. She'd worn it down today and the loose waves were held away from her face with her sunglasses.

"Did you have a good day?" he asked, doing his best to drag his gaze from her peach-colored lips to her big brown eyes. She'd grown more beautiful since high school, her trim build softened by fuller breasts and hips that were more alluring than ever. Though he'd always felt a basic appreciation and attraction, he'd never crossed that line for fear of jeopardizing their friendship.

"It was great actually," she replied, clearly oblivious to his distraction. "We had a pop quiz that led to an excellent discussion of what details students learn about our national history growing up in different parts of the country."

"You'd think we could teach national history the same way across the board," he said.

"Not in a country this diverse." She continued

walking and he fell into step beside her. "And there's never enough time to cover individual state history and national history. Although maybe my view is warped," she confessed with a smirk. "I definitely get too much enjoyment out of shocking them with the lesser-known details of Charleston history."

He laughed. That was so Allison. "If you don't have a kickback arrangement with the museums you should." He held the door for her at the end of the hall, inhaling her sunny fragrance as she slipped by. "I'm convinced you single-handedly keep them in business."

Her cheeks warmed with a rosy color that took him back to carefree summer days on the beach, surrounded by a crowd of friends. Those moments of complete freedom had gotten him through rough patches at home and helped him believe in a bigger life after high school. Helped him dream of something more than settling for the role of his dad's apprentice mechanic.

"I'll take that as a compliment," she was saying. "With these summer seminars, my primary goal is to light a spark and cultivate a lifelong habit of learning."

Her dress swirled just below her knees as they descended the stairs. He imagined anything Allison taught would spark something in her students. He had passed her classroom in session and paused to listen. She had such a passion for her topic, such enthusiasm in discussions that he felt like an interloper for even attempting to teach.

"Not sure my students are finding my class nearly as interesting," he said. In part because he didn't look nearly as appealing as *her*.

"I've seen you in action. Your students are fascinated." She shook her head, her glossy hair brushing her shoulders. "I'm still confused as to how you went from high school straight to the Marines only to come back to the Citadel as an instructor."

"The Marines have a way of putting you where they need you," he hedged. "I did get my bachelor's along the way."

She paused at the landing and cocked her head. "But you're out now, aren't you?"

"There's a window of time after you leave that gives them the option to call you back," he explained.

"They called you back to teach?" Her forehead wrinkled in thought.

Teaching was better than going back overseas, but why point it out? "That's what they needed." He shrugged a shoulder. "On duty or not, Marines are for life."

He opted to keep the new bodyguard gig to himself. In part because that's what the agency stipulated and also because he didn't want her to worry. She'd mentioned his safety in more than one of those Christmas cards.

"Did you hear about the baseball game tonight? I thought we could maybe go together."

Was she asking him out? The idea was more than a little enticing. When they were teenagers Allison had been the outgoing friendly girl with a wholesome kind of pretty that typical suburban moms wanted for their sons. Although it was impossible to know what his mom would have wanted since she'd walked out on him in second grade. Irrelevant now. He and Allison had met in fifth grade when she changed schools and had been fast friends ever since. By some tacit agreement, they'd kept it platonic and he'd brushed off the peer pressure to make a move or stake his claim on her.

He would never win an award for being the best at relationships, but even back then he knew treating women like property was the wrong approach.

"Just to be clear, is this a date?" he queried.

Her hair swung again as she shook her head. "No. Don't get all weird on me," she said, eyes twinkling.

"I'm not getting weird." Not a date. Smart considering she was his only real friend in town right now.

"The school reserves a block of tickets for the faculty for every home game," she explained. "I picked up two tickets this morning, assuming you hadn't heard."

A ball game would be a good opportunity to meet some other people and test his theory that he could be a normal civilian again. Some day. "Did I miss an announcement?"

Her lips curled up into a grin. "It's your first summer teaching," she said. "Those of us who make it an annual deal like to keep all the good stuff for ourselves."

"And leave the newbies floundering." He leaned back against the windowsill and studied her. The last twelve years had sure been good to her. "So much for that warm Southern hospitality."

She flicked her fingers, dismissing his mock-criticism. "Is that a yes or no?" she asked with a low chuckle.

His body reacted with a flash of heat. If he was talking with any other woman, he would've labeled that sound as sexy. But this was Allison, his best friend from forever.

"Yeah, I'd love to go to the game."

"Great." She beamed. "We're long overdue for a serious catching up."

"Sure." He couldn't share most of what he'd really

9

done for the Marines. Didn't want to. That was in the past and he was looking to build a future. If Allison was willing to be his guide to civilian life and contentment, he figured he was in good hands.

CHAPTER 2

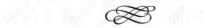

ALLISON FELT as if an elephant had been shoved off her chest. She could finally breathe easy knowing Logan would be at the baseball game tonight. She still had to overcome the nerves and get herself over to the ballpark, but she could do that. She was an adult, she'd be thirty in just a few months. She couldn't keep hiding from life like a scared little girl.

Wouldn't let her lousy ex-boyfriend keep that much power.

Although she wished now that she'd agreed to Logan's offer to pick her up, that would definitely have felt too much like a date. He was her friend. Granted, he was a friend who'd matured into a hot, sexy-dream inducing man, but that wasn't the point.

For a few heart-racing moments, Allison forgot all about the point, reveling in all the changes, from subtle to vivid. Logan's hazel eyes held a serious depth of experience now and faint lines she weren't sure were from smiling fanned from the corners. There was a small scar on the bridge of his nose. His shoulders had grown broad and layers of firm sculpted muscle filled out what had once been an almost lanky build. He'd been just over six feet tall at eighteen and he might've gained another inch, or maybe that was due to the posture and confident presence. The tight, clean professional Marine look had relaxed as his hair had grown a bit and a few days of beard stubble shaded his jaw. His mouth, tilted in that half-smile had always intrigued her, now it was an irresistible invitation…

She reeled in her wandering thoughts. He was her friend. Normally she didn't use her friends as human shields, but she figured Logan would forgive her. He'd stepped up and protected other kids against bullies in high school, surely he wouldn't mind doing the same for her tonight. And she would explain it to him, eventually, and find a way to thank him.

When she'd recognized his name on the faculty roster for the summer, she'd been so excited. She'd missed him during his military service. Worried for him. Other than a few random pictures on social media, she hadn't seen him in a dozen years. If she'd gone to their ten-year high school reunion on the slim chance he'd be there too, well, that was her problem.

In school, when anyone asked, she denied harboring any attraction to Logan. A small fib to protect something far more precious: their friendship. Watching him date other girls had piqued her curiosity and occasionally tweaked her temper whenever they used him for status or sex.

He rarely complained about anything, but when he did get hurt she was the only one privy to his confusion or sadness. Making it all the worse that now she was the user. She wasn't trying to make an ex jealous or make herself look better, but she did need a buffer.

Even so, shame chafed like a heat rash.

She vowed to tell him at the earliest opportunity, when they wouldn't be overheard. Logan would probably blow it off and say something about doing anything for a friend. He'd seemed remarkably happy to see her and willing to reconnect. Somehow that gap of loneliness between past and present had fallen away and they were right back in that comfortable, secure friendship she remembered.

It was nice and familiar and gave her zero insight into why she felt so different around him now. She gave her reflection a quick, stern lecture in the mirror as she braided her hair to keep it under control at the game.

"You're in a mood, that's all. Part of the break-up cycle." Six months ago her ex-boyfriend, Tanner Aultman, had shown his true colors. He'd slapped her across the face during an alcohol-induced melt-down after a big land deal had fallen through. She'd walked out and refused to speak with him again. So far, time and distance from that incident weren't enough. She still hadn't taken the risk of going on a solo date with anyone new.

Tonight was no exception to that recent rule.

"Logan isn't your date, he's a stable, helpful friend. And no matter how tempting, he is *not* rebound material." She grabbed her mascara and swept it across her lashes. "You have no business wrecking a friendship with inappropriate fantasies." Freshening her lip gloss, she stepped back for the full effect.

She'd hit the casual and comfortable target with her trim khaki capris and a sky-blue linen tank top. She had a jersey with the team logo to layer on when the sun set. Her favorite sandals and small purse were waiting by the door. All she needed was courage to leave the house alone.

Already, Logan was helping even from a distance. She couldn't leave him hanging with a bunch of coworkers he didn't know well. That would be rude.

The short drive from her condo on the Ashley River to the ballpark didn't give her time for more second thoughts. Once she parked, she waited until another group of people were passing by and used them as a buffer against Tanner. Her ex's company always had a suite and a crowd of people at the home games.

She made her way to the will-call box where Logan planned to meet her, relieved beyond measure when she spotted him right away. The weathered-red polo shirt and olive green cargo shorts might have been basic for any other man, but somehow the casual look emphasized his well-honed physique.

"Punctual," she said with a smile, trying not to stare.

His gaze traveled over her and her pulse quickened. "You look great."

"For a history professor?" she joked. In fact, the outfit wasn't too different from the more casual choices she wore to classes during the summer term. If Charleston knew anything, it was how to stay cool and fashionable.

One eyebrow lifted. "Still can't take a compliment."

He wasn't wrong. "Thank you." She didn't recall him sending many compliments her way when they were growing up. She handed him his ticket as they joined the crowd flowing toward the gate. "Just in case we get separated."

"I'm not planning on ditching my not-a-date pal," he said. "Just so we're clear."

She hadn't meant to offend him. Communication had never been a problem for them before. What would it take to stop overthinking every word? She had to get over this prickling attraction for him before she did something regrettable. Like kiss him, or worse, ask him to take her to bed.

Would she regret that?

He stopped at the concessions stand closest to their seats and bought a beer for each of them and a box of popcorn to share.

"Perfect ball game appetizer," she said, tapping her plastic cup to his when they stepped out of the line. "To good friends."

A ghost of his notoriously wicked grin flashed across his face. "Back in our Friday night football days, your go-to was a pretzel," he said.

"How do you know that? You were on the field playing the game."

"I had my sources," he said, with a wink.

"At least the beer is legal now." She snorted when he turned a shocked expression on her.

"You did not drink during those games."

"I had my sources," she said, echoing him. Laughing, she started toward their seats, her steps stalling out when she came face to face with the one man she'd hoped to avoid.

"Allison." Tanner smiled and her blood chilled. "How lovely to see you again."

He wore perfectly tailored black twill shorts and a loose cotton blue-striped button-down with the cuffs rolled back to his elbows and the collar undone. It was the fashionably easy look she'd admired at one time. Now she could see through the moneyed veneer.

"Hello, Tanner." She tried to edge around him, but he didn't budge, effectively trapping her between himself and Logan.

Tanner's gaze momentarily lifted to Logan and though his expression didn't change, she knew he was calculating.

"Back in the saddle so soon?" he asked. "I shouldn't be surprised."

She tried again to pass him, but Logan's free hand landed lightly on her waist, a steady, comforting pressure as he moved in closer. "We haven't met. I'm

Logan." He handed Allison his beer and extended his hand. "You are?"

"A man who learned my lessons the hard way with this one." A subtle sneer twisted Tanner's mouth, but he met Logan's offered handshake.

In a blink, the sneer twisted into pain and Tanner tried to pull his hand from Logan's. "Apologize to the lady. Right now."

Allison looked down and saw Logan using his grip to crush Tanner's hand. She couldn't work up any sympathy for her ex.

"Call him off," Tanner whined at her.

"He isn't a dog to command." She sipped her beer to hide her glee over his pain. It was small of her, but this might become her fondest moment with Tanner.

"Apologize," Logan ordered.

"Sorry, Allison," Tanner said through a clenched jaw.

Logan released him with a little shove and her path was clear. She hurried along, going straight to their seats after making sure Logan was behind her.

He indicated she should go into the row of seats first, leaving him on the aisle. "Who the hell was that?" he asked when they sat down.

"My ex," she replied. "We broke up a while ago."

Logan was quiet, his gaze on the players warming

up down on the field. She hoped he'd let it go, but he didn't. "Were you hoping to reconcile?"

"Hell, no."

"Does *he* hope to reconcile?"

She gave that some thought. In the few days following the break up, he'd tried to convince her that his lashing out was a fluke. He'd begged her to take him back, give him another chance. The begging was as uncharacteristic as the violent outburst. She refused to be swayed by any of his outrageous promises. When he finally accepted that she wouldn't change her mind, he'd started badmouthing her to their mutual friends.

Some of that had gotten back to her colleagues at work, thanks to the ever-so-efficient Charleston gossip grapevine and made life sticky for most of her spring semester.

"No," she said, answering him at last. "It wasn't an amicable split, that's all."

"You're sure?" His eyes were narrowed and she was sure he was seeing Tanner rather than the field.

She touched his hand, waited until she had his full attention. "I'm sorry we bumped into him."

"I'm sorry you dated an asshat."

The comment, delivered in such a flat, detached observation left her laughing. "Me too."

She opened her mouth to explain that her ex

wasn't the reason she'd invited Logan when several more people from the faculty arrived and the window for personal conversation closed.

Allison introduced Logan to the people he hadn't met and while everyone got acquainted, she periodically checked to be sure Tanner was up in his box, lording his advantages over the rest of the crowd. She caught him watching her once, but as soon as the game was underway, she was pleasantly distracted by the action on the field and the solid presence of her friend at her side.

"Need another beer?" Logan asked when one of the vendors came by.

"Water would be better, please." The event organizers had arranged for coolers of water and soda to be stocked at the back of their section. It wasn't as luxe as Tanner's typical suite setup, but this was a more relaxed experience in Allison's opinion. "Concessions will deliver a picnic for everyone at the end of the third inning."

"Seriously?"

His reaction surprised her. "Is that a problem?"

"No." He grinned and her heart skipped. "I wasn't expecting the full service. They really go all out."

"They do. It's great community building all around." She bumped her shoulder to his. "Kinda nice to be on the faculty side, isn't it?"

"Can you imagine if Mrs. Marsh could see me now?"

"She'd have to figure the odds first." He'd given the poor woman fits during math class in eighth grade. Logan never seemed to be listening to her lessons, but he always had his homework done and aced the tests. If there had ever been a student unlikely to go into teaching, it was Logan.

"Is she still teaching?" he asked.

Allison paused to cheer a double play with the rest of the crowd. "She retired a few years ago," she said as they resumed their seats.

As the home team got set for their turn at bat, Allison noticed a couple of women from their group heading to the restroom. If she joined them she wouldn't be vulnerable to another encounter with Tanner. "I'll be right back," she said, excusing herself.

She had to scoot in front of Logan and, as she passed, he touched her arm. His fingertips were light and warm, but her body soaked in the touch like a sponge. "Want an escort?"

"No thanks," she managed. "I'm good."

She hurried off before the effect of his fingers on her skin became evident in her face. This was Logan, her original best friend. The nasty incident with Tanner had clearly eroded more than her confidence in her judgment when it came to men. What was she thinking?

She wasn't thinking, that was the trouble. Since Logan had walked back into her life as part of the summer faculty, she'd had a hard time remembering he was off limits.

There was a blessedly short wait at the restroom and they were all soon heading back to their seats. A group of rowdy teenagers rushed by and Allison had to stop and step back or get swept along with them. Stepping back, she collided with someone behind her. The instant apology died on her lips as a hard grip caught her arm.

"You bitch."

The hatred in his voice startled her, until she caught the whiff of whiskey on his breath. "Take it easy." She forced a smile. "We're in public," she reminded him.

He gave her a hard shake, his fingers digging into the flesh above her elbow. She had to lean closer to him to ease the worst of the pain.

"*Nothing* is easy with you. Nothing. Does your new muscle-bound boy toy know that?"

"He's not—"

"Save it." Tanner dragged her away from the access to the stands, away from the safety of her group. "You and I aren't finished."

She smothered her protest in the interest of sparing herself more pain. Already passersby were giving him long looks. This was Charleston, and a local baseball game, if she screamed or showed the least bit of resistance, someone would react and offer to help. If he tried to lead her someplace private, she would do just that.

"Get your hands off of her."

Logan. The threat in his voice came through, despite keeping his voice low. He looked at her over Tanner's shoulder. "Thought this guy didn't want to reconcile?"

The panic in her chest eased at the sight of him. "He doesn't."

Tanner let her go with a little shove and Logan drew her close to his side, his hand resting with an unmistakable and misleading familiarity on her hip. "Even if he did, I don't. His wishes are irrelevant," she added, glaring at her ex.

"You heard the woman," Logan said to Tanner. "Get lost."

"Or what?" Tanner challenged.

"Restraining order is the next step," Allison inter-jected before Logan could make a threat Tanner might use against him.

"Like anyone on the police force would believe my crazy ex-girlfriend felt threatened by *me*. My reputation can outlast anything lies you throw at me."

"She has her approach," Logan said. "I have mine. How's the hand?"

Glancing down she noticed bruising across the back of Tanner's right hand from their first meeting.

Logan jerked his chin toward the stands. "Get on back to your suite and we'll all enjoy the game."

Tanner swore under his breath as he stalked away.

Looking down, she saw the angry red marks on her skin. Again. Her body trembled as embarrassment and fury surged through her in turns. She tried to get back to the game, but Logan stopped her.

"Allison," he murmured. "Let me see." He turned so her back was to the wall and his body sheltered her from curious gazes. He tested the range of motion at her elbow, scowling when she winced.

"Let's get some ice from the concession stand."

"I don't want to draw any more attention," she protested. "It's not that bad."

"Humor me," he said.

"Fine." She looked up at him and her breath backed up in her lungs. She'd never seen that concern in his hazel eyes aimed at her. Oh he cared about her and he'd always been thoughtful, but she'd never been on the receiving end of his *complete* focus.

No wonder the girls in school had craved his attention.

He made her feel precious.

She didn't hear anything but Logan's voice, couldn't see anything but his face. The typical scents and odors of the ballpark were gone. Only the masculine fragrance of his skin, warmed by the evening sunshine, got through.

Cocooned in the moment, in the shelter he offered, she never wanted to leave. "I've missed you," she blurted.

He held her gaze. "Same goes."

CHAPTER 3

LOGAN WATCHED THE BASEBALL GAME, maintaining the reserve and composure the Marines had drilled into him from day one. Inside, he was reeling from whatever the hell had happened back there with Allison.

So she'd missed him. A nice enough sentiment between friends. Why had it sounded like a ringing declaration? Hell, when she'd looked up at him with those big brown eyes, her mouth a sweet temptation within easy reach, he'd nearly kissed her.

And now he couldn't stop wondering how those luscious lips would taste.

Not cool. She trusted him as a buddy, a friend. He was experiencing some weird fallout from getting all protective after her ex had jerked her around. Making a move now would be a lousy idea.

This was Allison, making a move ever would be a mistake. He needed her friendship more than he needed kisses… or wherever kisses might lead.

The home team came up with a hot double play and ended the inning. They were up by one run and Logan rose along with the crowd to cheer encouragement as the team headed to the dugout for their turn at bat.

He allowed his focus to stray only as far as Allison and the conversation within their group. Fully aware of her ex brooding in the suite behind them, he refused to turn around. The jerk was staring daggers into his back, but Logan wouldn't give him the satisfaction of any kind of response.

It bothered him how easily Allison lied to the group about the ice pack on her arm, as if it was second nature to explain away random bruises. If the jackass's fingerprints showed up on her skin surely someone would press her for more details, but he suspected Allison was prepared to wear long sleeves for a few days.

Had Tanner been violent during their relationship, or had she been victimized by someone else between high school and today? He cracked his knuckles. A real friend would know the answer.

Nothing pissed off Logan faster than a bully. Tanner clearly had money to burn. Sometimes that lofty attitude filled a person with a sense of entitlement and they didn't see any reason not to do whatever they wanted, whenever and however they pleased.

Well, Allison had an ally now and there would be consequences for Tanner if he didn't back off. Painful consequences.

During the 7th inning stretch, he caught Allison peeking over her shoulder at Tanner's suite. "Stop," Logan ordered under his breath. "Don't give him the satisfaction of thinking you're worried."

He pulled the icepack out of the cooler and handed it to her. "One more round before the game ends," he instructed. Probably overkill, but he didn't want her to suffer a moment's extra pain. She had to drive home unless he could convince her to let him handle that.

"I'm worried about *you* not him," she said.

He chuckled. "He didn't lay a hand on me. And he won't."

"That's not what I mean." She wrinkled her nose. "He has other ways of throwing his weight around."

"Still not worried. You'll have to elaborate." He draped an arm across her shoulders and pulled her close for a half hug, ignoring the blast of cold as the ice got squeezed between them. "After the game."

"He *isn't* the reason I invited you along tonight," she said.

He looked down into her upturned face and got sucker punched by another powerful urge to kiss her. Why couldn't he remember this was Allison? He was the president of her friend zone and probably the longest-running member.

All around them fans sang *Take Me Out to the Ball Game* along with a local celebrity, but he and Allison were once again caught in a weird bubble of privacy. Her tongue slid over her lips and her eyelids fluttered. He felt her breath catch as his gaze fell to her mouth.

Not a date, he reminded himself. Shifting away from her, he broke the spell that had fallen over them. "Need another water?"

She blinked a few times and her brow puckered over those dark eyes. "Um. Sure. Please."

He scrambled to the coolers at the back of their section and returned to his seat as the bottom of the seventh inning got underway. When Allison was locked onto the play again, he pulled out his phone and sent a text message with Tanner's name and the picture he'd taken before intervening to Jenna McRae. She was the research and technology assistant he worked with during his cases with the Guardian Agency.

When he separated from the Corps, he'd entertained offers from several private security operations. A few were ready to send him back into questionable territories or downright hot zones. Not what he was after. If he was expected to conduct business in sensitive places, he wanted clear orders and he needed to trust the people giving those orders.

A team in Montana, Brotherhood Protectors, under the guidance of Hank Patterson had reached out to him as well. He had a couple friends who had gone with them, but he really wanted to stay closer to his roots in South Carolina.

So when the law firm of Gamble and Swann invited him for an interview, he'd been all ears. As managers of the Guardian Agency they handled private investigations as well as personal security for a very selective clientele. Their unique set up intrigued him and they were understanding about the possibility that he might get called back to duty. The bonus was that he could relax in Charleston and get acclimated to civilian life at a pace he remembered. It had been the right choice, especially after the Marines exercised the call-back and assigned him to this summer teaching gig.

And reconnecting with his best friend had felt as

if the universe was giving him points for good choices, if not always stellar behavior.

His phone vibrated in his palm with the text reply: New client?

Possible threat to an old friend, he sent back. Best to get that out right away. He and Jenna had only worked two cases so far and hiding the facts wouldn't earn her trust. Please see what you can find, he added.

If Jenna's search turned up anything that implied Tanner was a threat to Allison, Logan could take that to the attorneys in charge of the agency and sort out an arrangement. Bottom line, he would not let anything happen to her.

Cheers erupted as the home team claimed the win with three straight strikeouts in the top of the ninth. When the fans started clearing out, Logan made sure he and Allison were in the middle of the faculty group as they headed for the exit. He caught Tanner watching them from his suite, but that was it. Maybe he'd gotten the hint at last.

"Why don't I drive you home?" he asked when they reached her car.

"You're acting like I've been attacked," she protested. "The way he grabbed me wasn't comfortable, but—"

"You were scared of him."

"No." She folded her arms over her chest, one hand covering the bruised elbow protectively. "I had a plan."

"Give him enough rope to hang himself?" Anger flashed through his system again, recalling her pale face and the fear in her eyes just before he stepped in.

"I deserve more credit than that, Logan," she said, her voice sharp. "He caught me in a crowd. I wasn't alone. If he had attempted to drag me out I would've screamed and fought to get free. He's moody and mean at times, but he's mostly harmless."

Mostly? "He's bigger than you," Logan pointed out.

"Not much." She flicked a hand in his direction. "He's not built like you."

Was that a compliment? Her cheeks flamed with color. Damn. It *was* a compliment. He lost the battle for composure and grinned down at her, a little smug and a little too intrigued.

"My point is that I know how to take care of myself," she said, each word clipped. "Been doing it for some time now."

"I'm sure you're all kinds of capable, Allison. Nothing makes me happier." But his molars were grinding. Tanner was off and he couldn't shake the sense that she was at risk, despite all her assurances. "Humor me anyway and let me drive you home."

She rolled her eyes. "Logan."

"We're friends, right?"

"What about your truck?" She was relenting. "You can't leave it here."

"I walked over."

"What?" She looked around. "You're kidding. From where?"

"The summer teaching gig came with a rental house a couple blocks off campus."

"That's a long walk." She twisted around, looking back toward the Citadel, though it was too dark to see it right now. "Wait. You're only here for the summer? I thought you were back to stay."

The parking lot was clearing out quickly but this wasn't where he wanted to be alone with her, not with her ex in the vicinity. "How about we do some of that catching up deal on the drive to your place?"

He held out his hand, pleased when she finally dropped her keys into his palm. He walked her to the passenger side and opened the door for her. Once she was situated, he closed the door and scanned the parking lot, grateful Tanner was nowhere in sight.

When they were inching along in line with the other cars he said, "Allison, you should know I'm more than a temporary teacher and former Marine."

"Almost former Marine," she joked.

"True enough," he agreed with a smile. "My point is, I do plan to stay in Charleston. I've got some things lined up."

"Things, like job options?"

"Yes. If you're having serious trouble with your ex, I might be able to help make it clear that he's not welcome in your life."

"That's... generous," she said. "But he's just annoying, I promise."

"How did you guys meet?"

"This wasn't exactly the catching up I had in mind," she muttered. "At the College of Charleston, actually," she said at last. "He was the guest speaker for the business program convocation. I bumped into him in the hallway on his way to the reception that followed."

Tanner's possessive and bullish behavior with Allison left Logan wondering if that meeting was as random as she believed. No evidence that he'd used her or set her up, so better to shut down any crazy theories until he had facts.

"He was charming at first," she continued. "It took a little while for his true colors to show. But when they did, I walked out."

"Not great for his ego," Logan said. He'd met men like her ex. Powerful, connected and controlling, they often believed they were above the rules. They definitely didn't appreciate anyone else calling the shots or setting limits.

"Yeah." She sighed. "His bruised ego was a thorn in my side for a while."

"How so?" If she was downplaying what this bastard had done he was going to take action with or without approval from his new agency. The way the man looked at her set off all kinds of alarms in Logan's head. Tanner had demonstrated the kind of focus that bordered on obsessive.

"I didn't ask you to the game to deal with him, I promise."

"That didn't even occur to me." Traffic slowed as the light changed to red and he glanced over at her.

"I'm not sure why he won't move on. We don't run in the same circles. I'm no real threat to his pride." She fidgeted in the seat, her gaze darting to him and then away. "It's true I expected him to be here, but I don't want you to feel used."

Where was all this coming from? People had used him, from his dad to more than one girlfriend through the years, but Allison had never demanded more than he wanted to give. "You're my friend," he said. "If I can be helpful, I will be. He seems like trouble to me, Allison."

She turned away from him, staring out at the historic city passing by her window.

"Hey." He reached over and touched her shoulder, smothering an oath when she jumped. "Just me," he said. "Since I left the Corps, I signed on with an agency that handles private investigations and security. They recruited me, and agreed to my request to be based here in Charleston. They have loads of resources."

She swiveled to stare at him. "You're a bodyguard."

"Unthinkable, huh?" The way she studied him so intently made his temperature rise and filled his mind with sexy ideas he'd never before put in the same box with 'Allison the best friend'.

"No, I can see it," she said in a breathless rush. "Too easily. You were always protective."

"I was?"

"Yes." She laughed. "Have you never looked in a mirror? I used to get so aggravated when the girls hanging all over you would take advantage of your mile-wide protective streak."

He wasn't sure what to say to that so he kept his mouth shut, following a lesson learned early in his military career. "All right, moving on. The agency I work for doesn't advertise, but you know me and, as my friend, you have an in. They have incredible resources."

"Tanner is unhappy, that's all. He's unhappy with me because I didn't put up with his crap." He caught her chewing on her lip before she continued. "And because I'm a historian with a focus on the local area. Last year, before we broke up, I found something that could impact one of his planned developments. My work has already been delivered to the historical society, but he's been asking me to double check my findings. He wants me to pull the report and tell everybody I was wrong about the historical significance of the site."

"Are you wrong?"

"No."

Even with that piece, it still didn't quite add up. He'd picked up some very personal vibes at the ballpark. Granted, he didn't know all the players or the full background, but he wasn't about to leave her hanging. "So this little stunt at the ballpark is a common event?"

"No."

That didn't ease his mind much.

"Logan, I'm sure he was only trying to rattle me so I'd cooperate and retract my report."

Logan was liking this less and less with every passing minute. "He's threatened you?"

"He's too smart to make outright threats. He skirts around it. When we first broke up he tried to get me back. When he realized that wouldn't work he made noise about the quality of my research. When that didn't convince the powers that be to side with him, he went away for a little while."

"Went away?"

"He traveled for a couple of months, according to the rumors I heard. He invested time and money in other projects. I didn't want the details."

"And now he's back?"

"Yes. My six-month reprieve seems to be over. As I said, my research is already part of the historical society record. I included plenty of anecdotal material to corroborate my work. Now the parcel he had planned to develop into luxury condos on the Cooper River will soon be listed as an historical landmark."

"Preservation is what you always wanted to do with your life," he said.

"Damn straight."

Her smile, glowing and full of pride took him straight back to when they were kids, dreaming of all the things they would do when they were out of school and on their own.

He supposed they had both hit most of those goals. She'd become a professor, sharing her passion for the past with others and spending her free time in public and private libraries pouring over old books and diaries. It was so Allison.

And he'd bolted, eager to discover the world beyond the South Carolina Lowcountry. Freedom from those heavy expectations was all he'd ever wanted. It hadn't all been sweet tea and sunshine, but he'd carved that adventure through his own efforts, shedding his past. Overall, he enjoyed his service and the people he'd met, but he was happy to be home. He might even be content once he figured out where and how to fit into civilian life.

"You're going to look into Tanner no matter what I say, aren't you?" she asked as they drove over the bridge that spanned the Ashley River.

"I am." He wouldn't lie to her. "Can't help it. Maybe you're used to the man's face, but I didn't like it. You mentioned his true colors. Why did you break up?

"He hit me."

Her tone was bland and practical, as if she was relaying a universal fact: *'He hit me.' 'The sky is blue.'* Her detachment scorched his senses and he wished he hadn't exercised any restraint at the ballpark. To hell with the consequences of pissing off a rich bastard with connections.

"I'm sorry he hit you," Logan said. He needed to

get that out there first. Spouting off about how badly he wanted to pound on the sorry excuse for humanity wasn't helpful for her at this point. It was over, and it sounded as if she removed herself from the situation immediately.

"I'm not after your pity," she snapped. "As my friend I would've thought you knew that."

"Compassion isn't the same as pity." He struggled to speak through his tightly clenched teeth. "Someone struck you. That isn't cool and it isn't all right."

"But I'm supposed to be all right with you wanting to go beat the crap out of him for it?"

He let that go unanswered as he drove through the open gates of her condo community. How could he explain this worry for her when he didn't quite understand it himself? It was all in his gut. At the moment all he knew was that he didn't like the way Tanner looked at or spoke with Allison. That wasn't even close to reasonable cause to open an investigation.

She reached out and touched his arm when he parked her car in the space she'd indicated. "I'm not trying to be difficult. I invited you out tonight so we could catch up as friends. Just you and me."

"Your problematic ex had a suite almost directly

behind our seats. Sure you weren't hoping I'd be your buffer?"

"Fine. Yes, I did hope your presence would keep him away tonight. But I don't need a full-blown bodyguard, Logan. He's a nuisance, that's all. I ended things the same night he hit me. The experience was awful, I won't deny it, but I'm glad his mean streak came out when it did. His stunt saved me from wasting time."

He adored Allison, but he wasn't quite buying all this confidence. He'd seen the wariness in her gaze and her fear-pale face when Tanner had touched her tonight. The incident that ended their relationship still affected her.

"Did you report him for assault?"

"No." She stared down at her lap. "The bruising on my cheek was minor. He was drunk and there just didn't seem to be much point in doing anything other than walking away."

"Were you in love with him?" Was she still?

Her head came up and her eyes went wide. Maybe he should retract the question, but he let it hang there to see how—if—she'd answer.

"No, I did *not* love him," she replied, her gaze steady on his. "His lifestyle was a blast and he was fun to date until he wasn't."

"Did you ever talk about your work while you dated?"

"Of course." Her eyebrows pleated over her slender nose. "I don't recall ever speaking directly about my research conflicting with his planned development."

"What about rumors that he had violent tendencies?"

"Not that I heard before or since that night," she replied. "Once I walked out and he gave up on winning me back, his faulty relationship skills weren't my problem." She paused, her eyes big and dark in the dim light of the car. "If I wasn't your friend would you be this interested?"

"I would definitely be interested in every detail if you were a client. We've taken cases like yours where someone who thinks they've got some claim or right to bully another person.

"I haven't been a private sector bodyguard for long, but I know my way around providing general security. I also know how to do the job without making it obvious to anyone else. You need someone to keep that jerk away from you. Why not me?"

Her silent reluctance spoke volumes. He'd pushed hard enough for one night. Climbing out of the car, he went around to her side and opened her door.

When she had her keys and had locked the car, he walked her up to her door.

"Look," he said as she fished her house key from that tiny purse. "I'll be around the school anyway, so you're covered there. I'm only a phone call away, Allison, whether you want to catch up or whether you need a buffer or whatever else comes to mind, I'm yours."

She stared at him for a long moment that gave him time to think about kissing her. Then she slipped inside and closed the door between them.

Logan walked away, knowing he wasn't done with her ex. She couldn't stop him from keeping an eye on her, but the decision for him to actively help had to be hers.

CHAPTER 4

ALLISON FLIPPED the deadbolt on her door, mostly as a signal to herself that she should stay put. She couldn't seem to walk away. For long minutes she stood there, her forehead resting on the door, wishing for Logan. Wishing for the impossible.

Whatever comes to mind.

His words had sent her imagination racing into dangerous territory. Since Logan had walked into her world she couldn't stop thinking of him in ways that weren't appropriate for best friends. He had just grown more handsome with age. There was a rugged confidence in the way he carried himself that tempted her to lean in. Doing that would lump her in with all the other girlfriends she'd watched him with during high school. Those who used him as some sort of status symbol to look better or make an ex-boyfriend jealous.

She didn't want to make her ex jealous. It would be ideal if Tanner would forget she existed. Not much chance of that now.

Tanner was used to having things go his way from business deals to women and everything in between. He'd been scared she would report the assault and the blowback would damage his reputation, so he'd gone on the offensive, badmouthing her. It had made for some awkward conversations, but her closest friends and professional associates seemed to ignore his insinuations, chalking it up to typical breakup frustrations.

In the kitchen, she set her purse on the counter and peeled off the baseball jersey, taking a look at her elbow under the bright light. The bruises were starting to resemble fingerprints. Damn it.

She retrieved the bag of frozen peas that she used for an ice pack from her freezer and wrapped it in a dishtowel. Walking out on to her balcony, she sat down in the chaise and let the sultry night glide over her as she massaged her aching elbow.

Her view of the river, night or day, soothed her. Living here reminded her how far she'd come from that quiet suburban upbringing a few miles north and west of Charleston. She might not have the husband and kids she'd expected by this stage in her life, but she was generally happy and content. She had work that inspired her and kept her enthused so she could, in turn, pass on that excitement to her students.

Thinking of her students, staring across the water to the shadows of the Citadel perched on the opposite bank of the river brought her thoughts right back around to Logan.

He'd been so careful, his touch deliciously tender when he examined her elbow. The immediate temper in his hazel eyes had faded, as concern for her wellbeing took over. She was a fool to entertain the hope that he shared this new-found interest she felt for him. Her crazy, sudden lust would wreck everything she valued most about their friendship.

When exactly had forearms become so enticing? She didn't have an answer, she only knew that Logan's obvious strength made her want to hang on for dear life. Forever.

She was a mess. She hadn't ever been this flustered around a man. Never around Logan. He'd changed so much, the physical attributes were only the start. She couldn't imagine what he'd seen during his career. She imagined he'd spent the years since high school fully engaged in the present moment and working toward a greater purpose for a safe, strong tomorrow.

She'd spent her time looking back at the people and places that had lived long ago.

So what was it that had changed in her, when she looked at Logan? She'd almost kissed him tonight and she was starting to regret that she hadn't. The most likely explanation was that he was *safe*. No, she'd never been in love with Tanner and that one hard strike wasn't on the same level as an over-whelming assault or the long-running abuse so many other women suffered. In that, she'd been lucky.

It was easier to convince herself she was fine when Tanner wasn't around. So she had ignored the counselors and other resources available at either college, determined to just work through this emotional mess on her own.

But she couldn't keep lying to herself. The incident had hurt far more than her face and her pride. Six months later and she had yet to work up the courage to go out on a date by herself, not even to meet a new guy for a coffee.

She glared out at the night, resenting the way she'd relinquished that piece of herself, that innate confidence, to a jerk like Tanner. There had to be a way to silence the doubts and the wariness that crept in on her at the mere thought of being alone with a man.

If she could erase Tanner's interference from the evening, going to the ball game with Logan had been a pretty nice outing. Not a date, but a good time with a friend she'd missed.

Maybe, if she was completely up front with Logan, he would agree to help her. She wouldn't presume he wanted to actually date her, but a few practice dates would give them a chance to catch up and give her safe practice at controlling her new anxieties.

LOGAN USED a ride share to get back across the river to the house the school provided for him. It was less than a ten minute drive, but he was edgy, his mind on the threat he sensed from Allison's ex and his body aching for something far more interesting from Allison.

He didn't dare call the agency or check in with Jenna when he could be overheard.

When he reached the house and was alone, inside, he threw the deadbolt and paced for a few minutes. He wanted to get the short list of facts and his impression of the situation clear in his mind before he began what could prove to be a difficult phone call.

Charleston was an hour ahead of Chicago, but even if it had been the middle of the night, Logan had learned someone would always answer at the law firm of Gamble and Swann. When he was transferred, he was surprised to hear Gamble's mellow voice. Didn't the man have a personal life?

"Hello, Logan. How's it going?"

"Good, sir," he replied. "Things are pretty quiet and I'm glad to be back where it feels like home."

Well, sort of like home. He glanced around the front room of the simply furnished house. The oversized couch and chair, spaced around the oak coffee table gave a welcoming, comfortable southern vibe, but, aside from his clothing, nothing here belonged to him. As soon as he figured out where he fit in, everything would feel exactly right. But that wasn't Gamble's problem to solve.

"You can drop the 'sir,'" Gamble reminded him.

"Sure." Some habits didn't break easy. "Hey, I, *um*...bumped into a situation," he began. "Possible situation. An old friend from high school could be in trouble. I'd like permission to take myself off the on-call status and look into it a little closer."

"And you'd like to look into it with our agency resources?" Gamble asked.

Maybe Jenna had filled in their boss. Logan didn't mean to overstep or assume anything, but Allison deserved the absolute best he could provide. "Yours are the best resources I know," he said. No flattery here, just simple fact. He hadn't been with the Guardian Agency long, but their ability to grab good intel—and grab it fast—had impressed him.

"I'm listening."

"She ended a somewhat serious relationship several months ago, but the ex is harassing her. Something is off." He wished he had hard facts. "He hit her, once, and she was done. He tried to get rough with her tonight, but there's another layer. She did some research that shut down a big land deal and—"

"And you feel about this friend how?" Gamble interjected.

"She was my best friend through school. We've never dated and don't have plans to do so." Finding her sexy as hell wasn't the same as planning to date her. He was just getting to know her again. "This guy is all entitlement and ego. It's in the way he looks at her." Logan felt himself floundering. He should've done more on his own before making this call. "You've had me run a couple protection details now and I've got plenty of observation and analysis experience from my Marine Corps days. If you say no, I'll back off and just keep an eye on her, casually. To be honest it makes me nervous to think I might be on another case when he comes at her again and she needs my help."

"Has she specifically asked for help?" Gamble queried.

"No, sir." Logan winced. "No, not specifically."

Allison had invited him to the ball game as a buffer, but he suspected her ex had other motives for giving her grief. She was smart, but everyone had a blind spot, especially when awkward relationships were involved. And ostrich behavior was named that way for a reason. Plenty of times people ignored warning signs because it was easier than facing trouble head on.

"Give me the name of the man you're worried about," Gamble said.

His shoulders relaxed. He hadn't been fired or told off yet. "Tanner Aultman," Logan reported, his fingers reflexively curling. He bounced his fist lightly on the top edge of the couch, hoping the wait wouldn't be long.

The agency seemed to make swift decisions with confidence and send out orders accordingly, something Logan appreciated. The worst part about his military career was having a gut feeling about an operation and then being stuck, waiting for the authorization to move.

"I'm not seeing any reports of violence or domestic trouble."

"She didn't report it at the time because it was minor and she was done with him anyway."

"I understand." Gamble mumbled something under his breath. "Serious money in his portfolio and he's listed as the majority partner on two significant and recent deals in Florida."

So why was he back in Charleston giving Allison a hard time?

"You think it is more about money than the personal issue?"

"Could be." Gamble was quiet for a long moment. "Why don't I give you a week," he said at last. "You were on limited availability anyway with your current teaching schedule. Go ahead and dig into the history between Aultman and your friend. Ask Jenna for help, if you need it."

"I can't necessarily promise that she'll become a paying client," Logan said.

"We'll cross that bridge when we get there. I'll let Jenna know you might be reaching out with more details."

"Thanks, Mr. Gamble. I appreciate the leeway here."

"We appreciate your excellent skills and solid work on your previous cases. You'll find, in general, we're an understanding team. Just keep us in the loop."

"You got it. Thanks so much." With a promise to send regular updates, Logan ended the call.

Relieved to have official permission to proceed on Allison's behalf, he pocketed his phone and dropped his keys on the kitchen counter. For the first time since he'd moved to this location for what should be his final assignment as a Marine, he didn't feel quite so out of place.

Now he just had to make sure Allison was truly safe without getting distracted by all the new ways she made his pulse race. He wanted her in his life again. Keeping her as a close friend would be impossible if his sudden desire for her scared her off.

Charleston was full of beautiful women and he'd been out on a few casual dates since he'd been back. Unfortunately, he hadn't really clicked with any one woman in particular. So far, the women he'd met either wanted a fast hookup with a 'military hero' or they ran off because he had 'military baggage'. And not one of them had sparked such specific sensual fantasies with a smile like Allison did.

CHAPTER 5

ALLISON WOKE up the next morning with a mild ache in her arm and some stiffness around her elbow. Moving it gently, she decided it could've been much worse. Although the run-in yesterday with Tanner had given her plenty of unpleasantness to think about, she was determined not to let his antics derail her routine. The man was in her past, to hell with his opinion on the subject.

Today was her late day. Her first class didn't start until after noon so she dressed for the morning yoga class, pulling on a long-sleeve shirt over her usual tank top to cover the bruises. She'd be warm, but the class was held outdoors on clear days and there was always a nice breeze in the riverfront park of her condo complex. The many activities and friendly neighbors were her favorite perks of the community.

With the pool, nature trails and the boardwalk to a dock, being right on the river was almost as refreshing as a trip to the beach.

With her yoga mat under her arm and a water bottle in hand, she headed downstairs. The humidity met her head on as soon as she stepped outside her door, but she didn't mind. She loved everything about living down here. She and Logan had actually grown up further inland, but she'd spent as much time as possible in the heart of Charleston. All of the best, eclectic shops had been down here and the cute college boys were a big attraction back then too, she remembered with a smile.

"Good morning," the instructor, Charlie, said as Allison walked up. Charlie had that lithe yoga body that seemed built to form impressive pretzel-like poses. It was her smile, as bright and welcoming as sunlight, and her warm, patient guidance that made the classes a wonderful experience. "You look like you're in a good mood."

Allison grinned. "I had a really nice evening catching up with an old friend," she replied.

"That's great energy. So positive," Charlie said, beaming. "Let's build on that."

For the next forty-five minutes, with Charlie's guidance, Allison built on that positive energy from spending time with Logan last night. And when the class was over she felt limber and loose and thoroughly content. As she headed back to her condo, restored and refreshed, she convinced herself that all those flutters of attraction for him were just a byproduct of not seeing him in so long.

They were friends and he had done a very kind, friendly thing by stepping in to help her. That didn't mean it had to turn into anything more.

In fact, she wanted him in the friend zone. *Really*. That friendship had been a boon for both of them all through high school. Friendship worked. It was enough. Had to be enough. It had taken her years to break the habit of reaching out to him for everything when he'd joined the Marines. That alone quelled any lingering doubts or curiosity about how he would kiss her. His vanishing act had been like losing a piece of herself. A piece of her heart.

She didn't want to chance that pain again.

Feeling settled, she blended up a post-workout smoothie and sipped on it while she multi-tasked: icing her elbow while she checked email and reviewed her lecture for the afternoon class. No one had any urgent questions or concerns and, so far, she didn't think anyone was getting lost. Her summer classes were as intense as any others she taught, but without the typical pressures of the semester, her students often found them easier.

She headed to her bedroom suite to shower and dress for the day. Her elbow only ached a little as she dried her hair and she smiled at her reflection. Logan would be happy to hear that and she imagined his relieved smile as she swept on mascara and lip gloss. Good friend, she reminded herself.

But it was going to suck the first time she saw him with another woman.

That wasn't fair to him and she needed to get a handle on that hot prickle of envy before it wrecked the treasure of their friendship. Annoyed with herself, she took a deep breath and tried to reclaim that post-yoga calm as she gathered what she needed for an afternoon at the school.

Her cell phone rang just as she reached her car and she smiled when Sadie McClain's name and picture appeared on the screen. Allison had met the actress a few years ago when she was helping consult for a movie. She hadn't expected Sadie to be so personable and down to earth, but she was, and the women had become fast friends.

"Allison, I'm so glad I caught you," Sadie said in a happy rush. "Hank and I are in Charleston for a few days and I was hoping we could get together."

Sadie's husband, Hank Patterson, had been a Navy SEAL. When his military service ended, he'd returned home to Montana, reconnected with Sadie and founded the Brotherhood Protectors, a private security service.

It reminded her of Logan's decision to become a bodyguard. Meeting Hank could be good for Logan. They'd probably have plenty to talk about. She'd love it if her oldest friend in the world enjoyed spending time with her new friends too.

"I WOULD LOVE THAT," Allison replied. She stashed her laptop bag and purse behind the driver's seat and closed the door. "Just let me know when and where."

"We got in a few hours ago and are settling in at the resort. I have meetings this afternoon. Would you be willing to meet us at The Dive on Sullivan's Island for drinks and maybe some dancing? Tell me you've got someone hot and fun you can bring along."

Logan's face immediately popped into her mind and her pulse skipped happily through her system.

He was a *friend* and he'd be great company, but Sadie was hoping that Allison was dating again. She'd confided in Sadie when she'd first broken up with Tanner, telling her about the fight without sharing the full extent of his tantrum.

"I think a friend can join me. He's a great dancer,"

she added in a hurry. "Either way, I'll definitely be there."

"Friend." Sadie snorted lightly. "Maybe I'll make a few calls and see if a few more *friends* can join us."

"That's… sweet. But not necessary," Allison said, hoping to avoid any blind date awkwardness.

"We'll see. The Dive doesn't bother with reservations and the band tonight will bring in a crowd, so it's not really a problem either way," Sadie said. "I'm thinking seven-ish. I'll send you a text when I know for sure."

With the plan in place, she opened her door and sank into the driver's seat. A shadow fell across her as she reached to close the door. Looking up, she saw Tanner. A chill slid down her spine, settling like a ball of ice at her low back. It was all she could do to suppress the urge to shiver.

He'd caught her door and was holding it open. Silently she scolded herself for taking her safety for granted. She shoved the key into the ignition. She could always start the car and drive away even if that caused him some injury or discomfort.

"I was hoping we could talk," he said.

"I don't have anything to say to you," Allison replied. She looked around for his forest-green Jaguar he'd driven when they dated, but didn't see it nearby. Of course the man had several vehicles. How had he even gotten through the guard at the gate? She'd revoked his code when they broke up. "Please leave."

"Hear me out." He held firm when she tried to close the door. "I know I screwed things up Allison. I'm truly sorry."

"You've said that." Apologies or not she wasn't going back to a man who had already struck her. He'd been *her* first direct encounter with domestic violence, but she wasn't sure he could make the same claim. She had watched other women get caught in a cycle of pain, apologies, reconciliations, and more pain. She had escaped Tanner and would not give him another opening to hurt her again. "I have students expecting me," she said.

"They won't start the class without you."

His dismissive tone was razor sharp and as annoying as a rock in her sandal. "Without me, the class won't happen at all. You wouldn't keep a business associate from finishing a deal," she said pointedly.

"Business is exactly what I want to talk about," Tanner said. "Walk with me down to the river. I promise you'll make it to your precious classes on time. Knowing you, you're running an hour ahead anyway."

"Belittling my work isn't helping," she warned.

His tone reminded her of the majority of their arguments that his work trumped hers. She tugged hard on the door handle this time, but he didn't give in. "This is absurd, Tanner."

"You can spare me fifteen minutes after all the grief you've caused."

The land deal. Logan had been right to worry about her. "What are you talking about now?" she asked, playing dumb. "You caused *me* grief last night." And Logan handled it without embarrassing anybody.

"Your friend was a menace." Tanner aimed a glare at her building. "Is he here?"

She ignored that. "Things would have been worse for you if my friend had not intervened."

He laughed, but the sound held no amusement. "How do you figure?"

"I was about to scream and make a huge scene that would've drawn all kinds of attention and negative publicity for you."

"You flatter yourself, Allison. No one cares if I argue with a frumpy history professor."

"Go away."

"As soon as we talk. Come on. I don't want to have this conversation where anyone can happen by and overhear me."

"You flatter yourself, Tanner," she shot back. "You aren't nearly as recognizable as you believe."

He leaned close and she pressed as far back as the seat would allow. He didn't touch her, but the intimidation, the sheer fury and hatred on his face, scrambled her thoughts. Her breath backed up in her lungs. Whatever her escape plan had been, she was too frightened to act on it.

"You *owe me* this conversation." His lip curled. "Let's go."

"You first." Tanner suddenly lurched back, assisted by Logan who gripped the collar of his shirt. "The lady doesn't owe you anything."

In the bright midday sun, he looked like an avenging angel. She finally dragged in a real breath. No melodrama or overstating it, he'd appeared out of nowhere, pulled the shadow of Tanner away, and saved her. Again.

"What the hell is this?" Tanner shouted. "Get off me!" He twisted and threw a punch that Logan easily avoided.

"You're free to be a jerk anywhere else." Logan swiveled and suddenly Tanner was pressed against the side of her car. "Allison has made it clear she does *not* want you around. I suggest you respect her wishes."

"We have business." Tanner tried to smooth his shirt.

Logan folded his arms over his chest. "What kind of business?"

"Nothing that concerns you. I only need a couple minutes," he said to Allison. "Then I'll never bother you again."

"Never again starts right now," she said. With Tanner out of the way, she closed her door and started the engine with shaking hands. Trusting that he would back away from the car as she pulled out of the parking space, she put the car in gear.

In her rear view mirror she could see him shouting at the vehicle. She drove slow enough that she saw him turn on Logan. No. She would not let Logan fight all her battles and definitely not alone. She braked and rolled down her window. "Logan?" Her voice cracked, but she shouted his name again.

"Go on, I'm good," he said. His gaze tracked Tanner as the man stalked away. "I'll catch up with you at school."

She hesitated, unhappy about leaving him alone. "I'll be watching for you." He could clearly handle himself without any help from her, but this was her mess, not his.

What would she have done if Logan hadn't appeared? What had he been doing over here anyway? He'd told her the rental house was right next to the school. His showing up didn't make a lot of sense, but she was too grateful to dwell on it.

At the first red light, she dried her damp palms on her slacks and checked her rearview mirror, but she didn't see any sign of his truck.

If Logan didn't show up to the school within half an hour, she would call the police and point them straight at Tanner. She didn't care what kind of influence her ex had or how many donations he made to the community. The man was unreasonable, irrational, and aggressive. She'd made a serious mistake not reporting his earlier actions. It was high time she shined a light on his outrageous and threatening behavior.

CHAPTER 6

ALLISON'S EX WAS PERSISTENT, Logan had to give him that, as he followed the bastard to his car. Unfortunately for Tanner, Logan knew how to dig in when it counted. Last night, he'd asked Jenna to give him Allison's full class schedule and typical personal routine. Having worked with her for a few weeks, he had a pretty good feel for her habits, but he didn't want to miss something and give her ex another opening to harass her.

Good thing too. He'd come by to surprise her and take her to lunch, only to find Tanner in her face again. Temper and impatience challenged his self-control. He wanted to pummel this guy until he was a blurry stain on the ground.

"Is this just you not able to get over her?" Logan demanded. "She's made her opinion of you pretty clear. Didn't you learn it's always the woman's choice?" He had to figure out Tanner's fixation on Allison and put an end to this.

"She and I have history," Tanner said. "We have a common interest to sort out."

"There is no you and her, Aultman," he said, his voice low and menacing as he stepped in close again. "She's done with you."

Tanner puffed up his chest. Logan was unimpressed. "What do you know about us? She'll never settle for a brute like you after spending time with me."

"Settle?" Logan snorted. "You're nothing but ego and a great car and she knows it." Though it would only prove Tanner's point, Logan was tempted to show him exactly how much of a brute he could be. But Allison was his friend, first, last, and always and he wanted to resolve this, not make Tanner dig in. "Leave her alone," Logan stated. "You threw away any chance you had. If I'd been here when you smacked her around, you'd have one less hand today."

"Big threats from a small mind," Tanner said with a sneer. "I never touched her."

Logan pushed his sunglasses up to the top of his head, planted his hands on his hips and lowered his voice. "Don't call my friend a liar."

Tanner's eyes went wide. "I-I just need to speak with her," he stammered.

"Not happening." Logan folded his arms over his chest. "Get the hell out of here."

He wasn't worried about losing Tanner. Jenna had the man's registration for the sleek, luxurious silver BMW convertible. Then she'd gone a step further and linked up with the vehicle's GPS system. Tanner had no idea how easily Logan could follow him and prevent him from causing Allison more grief.

"She owes me a conversation, at the very least," Tanner insisted. "You're interference only delays the inevitable. She *will* talk to me."

"About what?"

So far Jenna hadn't pinned down any clues to Tanner's unflagging interest in Allison. On the surface, looking only at their recent interactions, the situation could be summed up as a disgruntled ex who refused to give up on a relationship.

People could be persistent about throwing themselves against a closed door.

Tanner didn't seem to be trying to woo her. If that was his goal, he wasn't using effective tactics. Sure, he might be so ignorant and self-absorbed that he'd never bothered to understand Allison or her preferences. It worried Logan, put an itch between his shoulder blades. His instincts were humming: this man was a danger.

Could he provoke Tanner into revealing his reasons?

"None of this is your business." Tanner said. He inched toward the driver's door, clearly hoping to make his escape.

"Wrong." Logan slapped a hand to Tanner's chest, pressing him back against his perfect car. With the top down, it would only take a little shove to put the man upside down in those leather bucket seats. "I've made it my business. She talks to *me*." He eased up just enough for Tanner to take a deep breath. "And she tells me she doesn't ever want to see or speak to *you* again."

Tanner scoffed. "You can't be with her all the time."

Obviously, the man had no clue about Logan's tenacity. "What if we made a deal?" Jenna's report said Aultman loved to make deals, especially when he was sure he'd come out on top. "I'll talk to her for you."

"And I'm supposed to trust you to give me the truth?" He rolled his eyes. "I'm not a fool."

Logan pretended to think it over. "I'll tell you exactly what she says, no matter what it is, in exchange for your promise to never go near her again."

He could practically see the wheels turning in Tanner's eyes. At his core, the man was a gambler. He had a gift for turning high-risk real estate deals into immense and nearly-immediate profits. He seemed to have a golden touch and had created mega wealth from average seed money.

Jenna's file on Allison showed her finances were far more straightforward. None of her money tangled with Tanner's. There weren't any wild deposits or withdrawals that would indicate she had done any investing with the snake. So why did he still hassle her?

As FAR AS he could tell from Jenna's research, Allison had simply made a mistake and fallen for this guy's charming exterior.

"You would talk to her for me?"

"I would," Logan said. "No problem at all if it means you don't ever come near her again." He rocked back on his heels. "Assuming you're not after something stupid like forgiveness. There's no excuse and no coming back from hitting her."

Tanner swore. "You don't know anything about our relationship," he said, lips curling into a snarl.

"I know it is *over*. You need to get that through your head before I'm forced to help drive the point home."

"That sounds like a threat," Tanner said.

"Now you're getting it," Logan said easily. "Sucks to be on the receiving end doesn't it?" He took a deep breath, forced himself to smile. "What'll it be? Am I gonna be your messenger or not?"

"Not." Tanner's nostrils flared. "I'll handle this business my way."

"Works for me." Logan rolled his shoulders and took a step back. "Just as long as your way is far from Allison."

Tanner jerked open his car door and slid into the seat behind the wheel. "I can wait you out," he said. Then he pulled the door closed and drove off in a hurry.

Logan immediately called Jenna.

"Making new friends?" she asked.

"Looks like more enemies," he replied. "I suppose it's wrong of me to hope for torrential rain on a beautiful day."

"From what I've heard about South Carolina summers, odds are good he'll need to put the top back on that car sooner rather than later."

"How did you know the top was down?" Logan queried.

"Sugar, where there is a camera I have a view," she replied in a slow Southern drawl he'd never heard her use before. "You're friend's complex is at my fingertips," she added in her normal voice. "From the front gate to the dock."

"There's a dock?"

Jenna chuckled. "There is."

Nice perk. He hadn't been out on the water since his return home. Just the thought released the last of the tension gripping his neck. Allison's community was within Jenna's oversight. No need to spend another night awake and worried. Jenna would notify him even if Allison didn't.

"Any chance you have a guest code so I can get through the gate anytime?" Better to ask Jenna than Allison. He didn't want to pile on and upset his friend any more than she already was.

"I'll see what I can find. "You hoping to sneak in and surprise her later?"

Not a chance. "That kind of surprise would only upset her," Logan said. "She's more nervous than she wants me to know."

"Having your grumpy ex show up unannounced is never fun," Jenna stated.

"Something you want to share with the class?" Logan queried.

"Not at this time, thank you, professor," she said,

chuckling. "You better get over to the school before your class thinks they get the day off."

He checked the time and hustled across the parking lot to his truck. The Guardian Agency rules were clear that he and Jenna shouldn't meet, but he really liked working with her. She had grit and sass and he admired her initiative. She was more than willing to think outside the box. They'd only been on two cases prior to this situation, but already she seemed to have a feel for how he operated.

Confident Jenna would alert him if Tanner circled back, Logan called Allison on his way to the school. He had ten more minutes before her class was scheduled to start. Thankfully, she'd driven off when he needed her to go, but he knew she'd be stewing until she heard he was all right.

"Are you okay?" she asked, bypassing any greeting.

"All good here," he replied. "How are you?"

He heard her suck in a quick breath. "I'm okay. Thanks to you. Again. I'd really like to stop needing to thank you for running Tanner off. I swear I can handle my life."

"I believe you," he assured her. "You know I'm always happy to lend you a hand, especially while we're working together."

"Right."

There was a lengthy pause and he filled it before he lost his nerve. "Would you like to grab dinner tonight?" If she was just another case, he'd tell the client he needed to stay close and possibly gather more information. But this was Allison. His intent to stay close was far more personal than professional.

"Oh. Actually, um, I was about to invite you out. Friends of mine are in town and asked me to meet them at The Dive on Sullivan's. The band tonight is really good."

He hadn't been to The Dive in years. And having gone from high school straight to the Marine Corps, he'd never had a beer there legally. He smiled as the memories drifted through his mind. "The last time I was there I was with you. Out on the beach with a bucket of beer we bought with my fake ID."

"Oh my gosh that was—"

Her voice dropped off.

"Allison?" What now? He was less than five minutes away and there was security at the school, but it felt as if he was on the other side of the world. "Allison!" Had Tanner shown up to cause more problems?

"Relax. I'm fine. I just realized this wasn't a conversation to have in the lecture hall where our students could overhear."

His heart rate resumed a normal rhythm, only to

spike again when she laughed. The sparkling sound rippled over him, as if she'd dragged her fingertips across his skin. He really had to get this unruly attraction under control.

He tried to laugh with her, but the sound was rusty in his ears. "Guess we'll finish this conversation later. Are we going straight from work?"

"I know it's fussy, but I'd like to go back home and change first."

"I don't mind." He really didn't. "What time should I pick you up?"

"Six. That will give us plenty of time," she said.

"It's a plan." He caught himself before calling it a 'date'. Maybe this time she'd invite him in. He had this inexplicable urge to see her home, how she lived and decorated a place that was all hers.

When they were kids, her mother had been in a full-blown country décor phase, with a focus on muted blues and mauves and loads of woodwork and antiques. It had never struck him as her style and the few times he'd caught a glimpse of Allison's bedroom from the hallway, the room had seemed brighter and less cluttered than the rest of the house.

In his opinion, Allison was a coastal girl. Whether it was a sunny afternoon or a late-night walk, she'd always been more open, almost effervescent, during their beach treks.

"Hey, did you ever kiss Dale on senior night at Folly beach?" he asked. Making the turn into the parking lot, he took the space as close to her car as possible.

She sputtered. "Logan. Gotta run. Time to start class. You have a great day."

He was grinning ear to ear as he pocketed the phone and climbed out of his truck to prep for his own afternoon class.

CHAPTER 7

IT WAS strange to be heading back to The Dive with Logan after all these years. Everything felt the same and so different. The last time she been out here with him had been the weekend after spring break during senior year. They'd come out with a big group of friends for an all-day Saturday beach party. When she let herself think back on that day, bliss bubbled through her system.

They'd had so much fun that day. Yes, there had been beer by the bucket, even though they were all underage. But there had been bodysurfing and impromptu soccer games and warm sand under her feet. Scents of the ocean and sunscreen melded to all of it. Music and laughter, and nearly nonstop chatter as they all clung to what it meant to be on the cusp of the next step in their lives.

"You were dating Roxie when we were here last, right?" She didn't feel bad for asking after he'd mentioned Dale earlier.

"That's right."

"She thought you were going to marry her," Allison said as it all came flooding back.

His chin dropped. "She did not."

"You didn't know?" She chuckled at his obvious discomfort. "She had your first two kids planned and named."

"Stop it." He shook his head. "We were eighteen. She dumped me the next week."

"A test," Allison said with dramatic flair. "You failed, in case you were wondering. She held out hope right up to the point where you skipped graduation for Parris Island."

"That's nuts."

"Not really. She eventually married Dale. They have three little girls last I heard."

"No way." He laughed, but it faded away. "I couldn't have stayed," he said quietly. "I needed—"

"To get out." She reached over and rested her hand lightly on his arm. "You would never have felt complete if you hadn't gone and done something for you."

"You understand?"

"Always, even when I missed you desperately," she admitted.

His home life had been hard. His father was a good provider, but demanding and grim after his mom disappeared. Logan had told her once, out on the beach actually, that he'd only learned what happy meant by watching her and her family.

As he drove across the low bridge spanning the marsh, she realized she had yet to tell him who they were meeting. She'd spent the afternoon hoping that if tonight went well, it would be enough to restore her confidence. Then she wouldn't have to embarrass herself and ask him outright to help her get comfortable dating again.

Even if she did have to ask, they were adults. He was her best friend. They'd been helping each other through good times and bad from day one. It didn't have to get awkward unless she got all twisted up over the ways he'd changed. That was all physical. She'd always been the one claiming he should be respected and admired for more than his good looks. Logan's true value was his heart and integrity. His compassion. That was all the same.

It helped to remember she'd changed too and he didn't seem to be fighting any overpowering new attraction for her. "We're meeting Sadie McClain and her husband tonight."

"Sadie, the actress?"

"The same," Allison replied. "Her husband is—"

"Hank Patterson," he finished for her. "How do you know them?"

"We first met while I was consulting on a movie set here in town," she replied. "Sadie and I hit it off. We try to get together whenever they're in town." She did the math and guessed it was possible Logan had met Hank on a military operation. "Did you work with Hank?"

"No, we've never met," he said. "I've heard the name plenty, though. He's a legend. And his personal security business has a stellar reputation. They reached out to me when word got out that I was leaving the Marines. I have friends who joined his operation in Montana."

"Small world," she mused as the ocean came into view. The first glimpse of that vast water stretching to the horizon always stirred her. She rolled down her window and breathed in the salty air, heedless of the thick summer humidity.

"It can be." He rolled down his window too and then gave her a smile that made her toes curl. "How did the movie turn out?" he asked.

"I loved it," she said. Her heart fluttering in her chest, she looked away before he noticed the effect he had on her. "It had good reviews, too, so I must not have been too biased."

"That's cool."

"It really was a great experience. Sadie is so friendly and approachable. You'll like her. She and Hank are a wonderful team. I'll actually miss not seeing their little girl on this trip."

"Sounds like you're close," he observed.

"I guess we are." Allison's heart warmed at the notion. "I never expected to run in her circles, even occasionally. I'm a home town girl, you know that, but I admit it feels fabulous when my career opens up new doors and I like meeting new people."

She'd felt that way about Tanner for a time, lucky to have a wealthy and fabulous boyfriend who enjoyed going out and having fun. It was easy to scold herself for being fooled by him, but he was simply one dumb mistake among an otherwise flaw-less track record.

"How many other famous people have you met?" Logan cruised slowly along the main street, searching for a parking place.

Growing up, he'd had a huge crush on a young actress about their age. Now that woman also had lunch with Allison when their schedules meshed. "Are you still a Nikki Weston fan?"

"She's amazing." He braked hard as her meaning sank in. "No way."

"I won't tell you anything about her if you go all fanboy on me," she warned.

"You can be so mean," he accused. "Do Nikki and Sadie know each other?"

"Of course. They're close friends." Allison glanced his way, judging how much she could tease him. "Nikki spends more time here in Charleston than in Hollywood these days."

He found a spot and parallel parked the big truck like a pro. When he cut the engine, he stared at her. "Seriously? How do you know this?"

She gave a little shrug and a smirk. "Connections baby. History is a gateway to all kinds of great things."

"It is for you because you worked your tail off to be the go-to expert," he said.

She preened a little over his praise. "Come to think of it, Nikki met her new husband, Brett, when he was her bodyguard."

"She's *married*?"

Allison laughed when Logan slumped in utter defeat. "I'm sorry to crush your dreams, my friend." She patted his cheek. "I'll do my best to make it up to you on the dance floor."

He grinned. "I'll hold you to it."

The spark of heat in his hazel eyes sent a jolt of raw awareness straight through her and she was a little breathless when he came around and opened her door. He didn't mean it as any kind of grand romantic gesture, it was just his way. She pulled herself together, even when he took her hand as they crossed the street.

The music pumped out of the bar, drawing them in from a block away. They had a sound that was excellent for dancing and she was a fan before they reached the hostess stand at the bottom of the stairs. She gave Sadie's name to the hostess and they were directed upstairs. Logan guided her up ahead of him and she was wildly aware of him. She paused for the group in front of her and his fingertips landed lightly on her low back, sending a pulse of heat from that point of contact all the way through her body.

She suddenly wished she'd worn jeans. She'd chosen a flowy sundress for the fun of it while dancing, but denim would be much better armor against all that masculinity behind her.

At last the group moved forward and she and Logan followed, reaching the main level of the bar that overlooked the ocean. Her gaze went to the view immediately. The white lines of low rollers were illuminated by the lights from the beach as they washed into the shore.

Across the room, Sadie waved, a big smile blooming on her face. With her blonde hair scooped up into a ponytail and big blue eyes, she sparkled like the Hollywood star she was. Allison assumed the lack of fans pressing for her attention was thanks in part to Hank. He wasn't actively discouraging anyone, but the casual clothing didn't soften that confident former-SEAL poise. Working their ranch kept him fit. He looked as if he could jump back into active duty at any moment. It would take a brave soul to intrude on the couple who were clearly intent on enjoying an evening by themselves.

The location also factored into their privacy goals. The Dive was one of their favorite spots and the locals were accustomed to seeing Sadie and Hank around town. They generally respected the Patterson's space whether they were lounging on the beach, shopping, or hanging out here with a beer and great music.

Allison made introductions, hoping the band smothered the quiver she felt in her voice with Logan pressed close.

Hank extended his hand. "Logan. The one that got away. Good to meet you," he said as they shook.

"Beg your pardon?" Logan aimed a quizzical look at her, but she was no help.

She couldn't recall sharing anything about her

teenage feelings for Logan with Sadie. "Don't ask me." Allison held up her hands in surrender.

Hank laughed, his green eyes alight. "One of my men tried to recruit you and you shut him down quickly."

Logan grinned as he sank into the chair across from Hank. "A phone call. You made me a good offer, but Montana wasn't Charleston."

"Not home," Sadie said, nodding sagely. "The heart knows where home is." She leaned over and kissed Hank's cheek.

"Charleston has its charm." Hank's gaze slid to Allison and he winked. "I see why you turned me down."

Allison wanted to protest and quell the assumption that she and Logan were together like *that*, but the waiter arrived. The young man with tousled blond hair took their drink orders, blushing and bobbing his chin whenever Sadie spoke with him directly. It was adorable.

"The band is awesome," Sadie said to Allison. Then she scooted around the table, crouching close so no one else could overhear her. "The man is better. Girl." She leaned back, fanning her face. "Nicely done."

"Stop. We go way back. Friends since long before high school," Allison explained. She didn't need

Sadie's matchmaking ideas to fuel her own fantasies.

"That's almost exactly our story," she said, her eyes twinkling as she returned to her seat. "So you two never dated back in the day?" Sadie directed the question to Logan.

Clearly, Sadie was not giving up.

"No," Logan answered with a smile. He draped his arm across the back of Allison's chair. "She was too busy for me."

Allison shot him a look. That couldn't really be the reason they'd never tried to date. "More like we were too good as friends to mess it up," she said.

"Well last I checked you're not seeing anybody." Sadie wiggled her golden eyebrows. "Are you spoken for Mr. Logan Harris?"

"No, ma'am." He softened the moment with a broad wink. "I'm just here for the music. And to brush elbows with celebrity of the military and Hollywood variety."

The Pattersons grinned at each other as if that was some special inside joke, no one else would ever understand. "Do you dance?" Sadie queried.

Allison's heart went fluttery again. Oh, man could Logan dance. Some of her best memories were dancing with him at the beach or backyard parties and even school events. She still felt a little cheated he'd skipped that graduation ceremony and the party that followed. If she'd known their last dance would be the last dance, she would have treasured it more in the moment.

"Yes ma'am." Logan smiled. "Do I need to prove it? Assuming your husband doesn't mind sharing you for one song."

To Allison's surprise, after watching his wife take the dance floor with Logan, Hank invited Allison to join him. She popped up out of her chair, eager to do anything to take her mind off Logan. The band was playing a tune with a swing rhythm that was perfect for the beach shag dance steps so popular in South Carolina.

"You're surprisingly good at this," Allison said when the steps brought her close enough for Hank to hear her.

"Sadie's a good teacher. She loves this stuff."

This was one part of her life Tanner hadn't tainted. This kind of bar and band weren't posh enough for his tastes. She'd tried to teach him the shag, but he didn't have any patience for the moves and fought the loose flow of the pattern. Really that should've been her first sign that he was all wrong for her.

The more time Allison spent with the Pattersons, the more she believed in happily-ever-afters. Not that Logan should ever be more than her best friend, but something about their strong partnership gave her hope that her own Mr. Right was out there.

As the song ended, and blended into the next, they changed partners and Allison found herself dancing with Logan. Within a few quick steps, they were back in that easy synchronicity they'd always enjoyed as kids.

"Wow." She grinned up at him as the sweet familiarity rolled through her. The smile on his face made her breath catch, but it didn't affect her steps. They were as smooth now as they'd been all those years ago. "This takes me back."

He'd always been one of her favorite partners. His feet moved with a softness that belied his solid build and the touches as he guided her were so light, he made her feel like she was floating through the music. In the past when they danced, it had been the closest she'd come to wishing they were more than friends.

When the four of them returned to the table, she was flushed and warm from dancing in general and Logan in particular. They'd never kissed, but tonight she couldn't seem to stop looking at his lips, the strong column of his throat, and his hands. His knee brushed hers under the table and she doused the feverish sensation with a cold glass of water and quizzed Sadie about her upcoming roles. Better to focus on the food and conversation rather than the boy she loved as a friend and the man he'd become.

The man she was starting to find even more irresistible.

Sadie entertained them with stories about their daughter, Emma, as they dug into a pile of famous Dive nachos. Hank and Logan talked a little shop about military life and expectations in retirement, but she didn't hear all of it because she and Sadie were busy making plans and talking about when they could connect with Nikki too.

It was such a normal evening, and too damn easy to slip into the dreamy idea that she and Logan might be a real couple someday. She jerked herself away from that precipice time and again. She wouldn't damage their friendship by shoving him into a role he probably didn't want just because she was insecure. It wasn't his fault he was the only man she felt safe enough to be alone with. She finally relaxed, imagining his reaction if she came clean about all the things rattling through her mind. Thank goodness Logan understood what it meant to be a true friend.

"Logan, have you met Brett, Nikki's husband?" Sadie queried at the end of the band's set.

Logan shook his head. "Should we have met at some point?"

"I thought so. Hank told me you went with the Guardian Agency and he's one of their investigators. And a local."

"I'm brand new," Logan replied. "The only employee I've really connected with so far is Jenna."

Disappointment chilled Allison's skin. Was he seeing someone? He had told her no, so maybe it wasn't serious. It definitely wasn't any of her business. But she felt as if she'd swallowed a bucket of ice. Deep inside, she was offended and frustrated that he might be interested in another woman.

Which was exactly the right thing for him. Her newfound attraction to Logan was her problem. She needed to remember her place as his friend. Support, encourage, and listen.

"…they don't even share last names," Logan said.

"Pardon me?" Allison interrupted. "Why not?"

"It's how they protect the privacy of investigators as well as maintain client anonymity," Logan explained. "They don't advertise at all, just rely on word of mouth. They emphasized that we really are *not* supposed to know anybody else."

"That policy seems to be relaxing somewhat lately," Hank said.

Logan chuckled and stretched an arm across the

back of her chair again. "With your reputation I shouldn't be surprised that you know more about my new employer than I do."

Hank's slow smile was enigmatic. The expression implied there was a long story he didn't plan to share. "Your agency and mine have collaborated a time or two," he said. "You're working with good people, in case you have any reservations."

"Thanks, man. That's good to know."

"Are you digging into new research now that your old project has been completed?" Sadie asked Allison, deftly changing the subject.

"You're looking for an inside track on a new historical film," Allison teased.

"Maybe," Sadie allowed. "You know how much I love this area and I'm always scouting good project ideas."

"Well…" She glanced around the table and decided she was among friends. "I'm thinking about a research trip to Daufuskie Island. It's one of the lesser known treasures in South Carolina with a great art scene among other things. Their history goes back forever."

"Before Charleston became Charleston?" Sadie asked.

"Long before. It'll take a lot of trust and cooperation, assuming I can find anyone willing to talk to me about the settlements that predate the European arrivals."

"I don't think you ever told me what area your previous research covered," Logan said.

She recognized his attempt to gain more insight on Tanner's irritation with her, but she didn't want to wreck a lovely evening with unpleasantness. Plus, it wouldn't be wise to pique Hank's curiosity about her ex. He hadn't been Tanner's biggest fan the one night they'd shared a meal at Tanner's place.

"I was looking at some of the history of ferries and settlements further north along the Cooper River," she explained. "Everybody focuses their research on Charleston specifically, and there are plenty of historical records and ghost stories to go around, but as people moved inland, there are some fascinating facts we've overlooked about early life around here."

Thankfully the band started back up before she got too excited and subjected them to a lecture on the subject. They danced through a few more songs, indulged in great food and conversation, and when the band announced their next break, Sadie exchanged a long look with Hank.

"We should be going," Sadie said. "I have an early meeting in the morning. Forgive me?" She gave Logan and Allison a beseeching look.

"Nothing to forgive," Allison said. "I loved this. Thanks for calling."

Logan added his thanks as they settled the tab. At the bottom of the stairs, Hank and Sadie turned for their car, but Logan caught her hand. "What would you say to a moonlight beach walk?"

Her heart lifted. "It's not a full night at The Dive until there's sand between my toes."

Side by side, they walked along the boardwalk, over the dunes and slipped out of their shoes. The refreshing breeze off the ocean felt wonderful blowing through her hair and across her cheeks. The sound of the waves a persistent thrum that soothed her as they started walking toward the water's edge.

"I know why people leave," she said, "but this is what always draws me back."

"There are other oceans out there. Other beaches to discover," Logan pointed out.

"You're right. But this one is so comforting." She looked out into the darkness and rather than feel small or insignificant, she felt as if she was exactly where she should be. "Guess I'm a diehard homebody."

"Never." Logan shook his head. "You like adventuring through the past, that's all."

No one had ever put it in those words. She basked in the compliment. Count on Logan to make her feel as if her skillset and passion actually made a difference. "Did you enjoy your adventures with the Marines?" she asked.

"For a time, sure. But this is home. I just wish I could figure out how to fit in after being gone so long."

"Seems like you fit in pretty well," she said. "Your students love you."

"Is that so?"

"That's the word on the street," she teased with a smile.

"I enjoy it, but I'm glad it's short term. We both know I'm not cut out for teaching full time. What I'll be doing with the Guardian Agency in the months ahead excites me. But I do feel a little detached searching for that connection to civilian life."

"You're unhappy to be done with the Marines?" Her voice cracked as worry that he might exit her life again rippled through her.

"No, not unhappy." He gave her shoulders a quick squeeze. "Detached is the only word I can come up with. There's life in the Corps and life away." He stopped, pushing a hand through his hair as he stared out over the dark ocean. "I don't mean to be a downer. It's hard to know what to do with myself in the transition. I'm waiting for something to click and make life feel right again."

"Selfishly, I hope you hear that click here," she said.

His gaze snapped to hers. "Do you?

"Y-yes." Her heart hammered at the intensity in his gaze. "I've missed my best friend." There was a fizzing in her fingertips that wouldn't quit and a rush of anticipation. It was as if she was on a roller-coaster headed up and up and up right before for that first big fall.

"I missed you too." His voice was almost lost under the sound of the surf. Neither of them moved, but it seemed as if they were suddenly much closer. "I've had other friends, Allison. None of them were you. You seem to know me better than anyone and yet you stick around."

"Well, the reverse is also true. You always make me feel confident about what I'm good at." She hoped that made sense. "I'm grateful for your service, Logan, but I'm so happy to have you home."

She pressed up onto her toes and kissed his cheek. Then she lost her balance as the tide washed over her ankles and back out, tugging the sand from under her feet. Logan caught her. Of course he did. His strong arms banded around her waist and he pulled her close to his chest.

Without a thought, her hands went to his shoulders. For balance or pleasure, it didn't matter once she was touching him. Her lips parted as she stared at his mouth, her body heating with anticipation.

Finally, her mouth was on his. A lifetime of avoiding this moment had been worth the wait. Sensation blasted through her, leaving a scorching trail of desire. She gasped and his tongue swept across hers. The taste of him was instantly addictive. She pulled herself closer, her breasts pressed against the unyielding wall of his chest, eager to take everything he would willingly give as the kiss spun out.

CHAPTER 8

LOGAN, his arms and senses full of Allison, couldn't recall ever feeling this good. Damn. Where had all of this been hiding? How much time had they wasted? She was his best friend, a line he thought he shouldn't cross. But she was absolute heaven in his arms, her lips soft and hot. She tasted of wine and the spices from their meal. The raw fragrance of ocean salt was tangled in her hair as it brushed his cheek.

Home. Every taste, every scent, every sound she made was *home*.

His mind raced to keep up with his body, cataloguing every sweet point of contact. Her glorious curves invited his touch and he ran his hands across the dip of her waist up her ribcage, his thumbs brushing the swell of her breasts. Her nipples were hard and she arched into his hands. He wanted to explore every inch of her, all at once, to hell with how impossible that would be.

It overwhelmed him. *She* overwhelmed him. His best friend was sucking on his tongue. For the first time in his life, he wasn't sure what to do next. It was as if he had a high fever and that battle calm at the same time. He'd happily lay her down right here in the sand and satisfy the aching need clamoring for release. Not a good call without so much as a towel to protect her from the sand. Not a good call out here in public where anyone might walk up on them.

He boosted her up and she wrapped her legs around his hips, hands locked behind his neck. She blessed him with a sexy smile before brushing her lips over his again. Featherlight and soft, and blazing hot.

He'd been looking for a connection, waiting for that *click*. Good Lord, he'd found all of that and more in Allison's kiss. He could hardly tell her she felt like his anchor. It wasn't the most flattering of compliments. Not that he could come up with much of anything while he was on fire for her.

"Allison," he murmured her name against the silky skin of her throat. He should be asking her just how far she wanted to take this. He'd die if she didn't say all the way. Her decision. His job to honor that. To protect her.

She hummed deep in the back of her throat. He flexed his hips and pulled her right up against the erection testing his fly. Her head dropped back on a delighted gasp, thrusting her breasts up. How long until he could taste her flesh there, roll his tongue over the hard peaks of her nipples?

"You're beautiful," he said, though it sounded trite. She was *more* than beautiful. And he never expected to feel this way about anyone. Definitely not her. She was Allison, his best friend, the one person he could count on to never leave him or use him.

She thought she'd used him at the ball game, but from where he stood that was just one more thing a friend would do for the person who mattered most. He pressed his mouth to the pulse beating at the base of her throat, admiring the glow of moonlight on her skin.

"Logan, please."

"Not here, sweetheart." This was no place to take things too far with people milling about and plenty of crowds up on the decks of the bars and restaurants lining this stretch of beach. He slowly lowered her to stand, secretly delighted when she swayed into him. "I would really love to have you alone, all to myself," he admitted.

"I'd like that too."

"Would it change too much?" He swore when he realized he'd spoken those words aloud. The way he felt, he'd rather find out and then discuss how to move on after the fact. "I mean your place or mine?"

On a ragged giggle, she dropped her gaze to his shirt. Her fingertips played with the top button. "It would be impossible not to change everything if we... if we keep going."

"Is that a euphemism for devouring each other in bed?" he joked. The moment called for levity or he'd never be able to walk back to the car.

"I must sound like a prude to you."

"Not a chance. I know you better than that," he said. He ran his hand up and down her neck, then angled her chin up for another deep kiss. "I've always wanted to know what that felt like," he admitted on a whisper.

She lifted her face back to look at him, squinting a little as if it would help her see him better in the shadows. "You mean that? Y-you have always wanted to kiss me?"

"Consider it one of my regrets," he assured her. "But you were so important to me. I didn't want to cross the line and wreck everything."

"That's how I felt," she said, her eyes brimming with emotion.

"So what does that mean for tonight?" he asked. If she told him that he could spend the night loving her, he'd jump at the chance.

"Probably we should take it slow," she replied. "Make sure and lay the ground rules for this, umm, detour."

"You have a lot of euphemisms," he teased.

Picking up their shoes, he guided her back the way they'd come. With his free hand, he held hers, needing the contact as they walked back to his truck.

He unlocked the door and held it open as she hopped up into the seat. "I'm not going to push you on this, Allison. But the floodgates are open. I want you wherever you'll have me. Preferably a bed, but I'm open to suggestions." She giggled and he couldn't help but laugh along. "Aren't we both adult enough to handle whatever is happening here?"

"I hope you're right." She traced his ear and he gave in, kissing her long and deep.

Breathing hard, he managed to drag himself away. "Buckle up."

He closed her door and rounded the hood to the driver's side. For a split second he thought about having sex right here in the truck. He'd done it plenty as a teenager and, although it would be fun, he wanted to give Allison something special.

Wanted that special something for himself, too.

She might not give him more than one chance. And if he only had one night with Allison, a woman and friend he valued above all others, he was damn well going to make it unforgettable for both of them.

They didn't talk at all on the drive back to her condo, but she slipped her hand into his and left it there for the duration of the trip.

At her condo she waited for him to open her door, then they lingered there in the parking lot, kissing slowly. It was as though neither one of them wanted to screw this up by saying the wrong thing. Eventually, she pressed a hand to his chest and they walked up to her door.

Her gaze dropped to the keys in her hand. "Do you want to come in?"

"Hell, yes." He rested his hands lightly on her waist. "But not tonight."

Her head came up and her big brown eyes were wide, full of confusion. "What did I do?"

"You tempt me beyond reason." He smiled, waited for that confusion to fade and then he laid his mouth on hers. "I want you, Allison."

"Then have me." She ran her hands up and down his arms.

"Count on it." Her lips were full and rosy from his kisses and he'd never seen anything so wonderful. "If you still want me—this—in the morning—"

"I will," she vowed. Her fingers curled into his shirt.

"I sure as hell hope so." They both needed time to sort out what had happened on the beach and how they wanted to go forward.

"Logan."

She dropped her forehead to his chest and he breathed in the fragrance of her hair. Ocean and citrus and totally her. He massaged the back of her neck. "You mean too much to me to be hasty about this."

"I can't believe this."

"Me, either, sweetheart." He held her close, knowing he was going to be up all night regretting this attempt to be honorable.

"I should be mad at you."

"Probably," he agreed. "I'm pretty irritated with myself." With one last kiss he backed out of reach. "Call me if you need anything." She growled. "Anything else," he amended on a strangled laugh.

Walking back down those steps was one of the hardest things he'd ever done. Twice he considered turning back and begging her to let him in, but he managed to stay the course. Discipline was the key.

It was telling that he'd forgotten there was more going on here than a sexy new development with his best friend. He hadn't even watched for trouble on the drive back from the bar.

He texted Jenna for any updates on Tanner's background or movement. Within minutes, she sent back a GPS tracking report from the BMW along with a reminder that the man had more than one vehicle. She'd found a Jaguar and an SUV registered to him as well.

Logan studied the map, grateful for a distraction from this yearning ache for Allison. Tanner's BMW hadn't gone anywhere near The Dive tonight. Too bad that didn't make Logan feel much better. The car had left the house, traveled to Shem Creek and then downtown where it parked in a garage for the better part of three hours, and then back to the house.

He sat in his truck for a long time, just staring up at her building. Her unit was on the far side, over-looking the river, so he couldn't see her lights come on, but he could imagine her moving through her home.

Peeling that dress off her body and then the lingerie underneath. She'd brush out her hair and pull on... something. What did she sleep in? A night-gown or an oversized T-shirt? Nothing?

If she ever slept with him, *nothing* is what he would vote for.

Desire gripped him by the throat and more sensitive parts south of his belt. Damn imagination. The only silver lining he could see tonight was that when he and Allison did finally make love it would be worth the wait.

WHEN ALLISON'S alarm went off early the next morning, she sighed and stretched under the covers. She should be annoyed or at the very least somewhat dissatisfied, but all she felt was a sweet anticipation. The sun peeking through the curtains shined brighter, and as she rolled out of bed, she felt as if she was still floating on the music with Logan.

She'd had an evening out with friends. She'd enjoyed what had turned into a pretty amazing date. And she'd kissed Logan.

Under the spray of the shower, she remembered everywhere his hands had touched her. Next time it would be skin to skin, she promised herself. Maybe she shouldn't be so willing to change the dynamic, but Logan had been a fixture in her life for so long. Last night... nothing had ever felt more timely or right.

She drifted through the rest of her morning routine and straight through her classes. Settling behind her desk for office hours, she let her mind wander over what would happen when she saw Logan today. Should she kiss him or keep her distance? The real question was if she'd be able to keep her distance now that she knew what it was like to kiss him.

"Don't tell me you're in here daydreaming over that brute whose been hanging around."

Tanner. His superior tone shredded her happiness. She rolled her shoulders back and steeled herself for another futile attempt at logical conversation. At least she didn't have any students in her office to witness this.

"We need to talk," he said.

Frustration swelled through her and she felt her cheeks go hot. "You're a broken record," she observed. "This is where I remind you that I don't have anything to say."

"Then listen." He advanced and braced his arms at the edge of her desk, crowding her personal space. "You will retract or amend or do whatever the hell it takes to make that report you gave to the historical society go away."

"It isn't that simple," she replied with as much patience as she could muster. "We were together through a good portion of my research. Had *you* been listening to *me*, you never would've made that purchase with the intent to develop the property."

"I bought the property before you ever turned an eye to it. I'm the reason you looked at it at all," he declared.

Her first inclination was to argue, but his gaze was locked on her and full of raw malice. Her skin chilled and her hands went clammy. She'd never seen him like this. The danger signs made her cautious. "You need to leave, Tanner."

"No. Not until you give me what I want."

"This is my place of business and I am here for students who need me." She wished one of those students would show up and startle him back out of his temper and back into the cool businessman he was known to be.

"No one needs you," he barked, doing his best to make her cower.

She was done with being intimidated by this bastard. Though she wouldn't dare handle him alone. "I'm calling security." She reached for the phone on her desk.

He batted it out of her hand. Before she could process that or react to protect herself, he caught her wrist in a bruising grip and jerked her close enough that they were nose to nose.

"Hey, Professor Weaver. Everything okay?"

Relief flooded through her at the sound of Logan's voice. She peered around Tanner and tried to smile at the sight of her best friend filling the doorway. Tanner was trapped now, Logan would never let him go without paying some price for touching her. His hands were loose at his sides and she could see the resolve in his eyes, the hard set of his jaw.

Swiveling to face Logan, Tanner swore. "Are you everywhere?"

"He's a professor here," she said. "And a body-guard," she blurted.

Tanner gaped. "You hired a bodyguard?

"What I do isn't your concern," she stated. "Will you leave on your own or should he give you an escort?"

"I'll take it from here," Logan said. His shoulders seemed to swell and before her eyes he seemed to get taller. "You heard the lady. Since you're lost I'll give you a hand."

There was no doubt in Allison's mind that any hand Logan offered would be in violence. She wasn't even ashamed at the flutter of excitement that her ex might take a beating. A better person probably wouldn't be quite so bloodthirsty, but when it came to Tanner, she wasn't feeling anything rational or kind.

"I'm the one with all the resources," Tanner reminded her with a snarl. "My resources can outlast your nonsense. Construction will start right where I want it to, rendering your precious historical site null and void."

"That's enough," Logan declared. "Let's go."

On a string of curses Tanner tried to barrel past Logan, but Logan made it impossible. Without saying a word or laying a hand on Tanner, he made it clear what he was choosing to go up against.

At last Logan shifted just enough for Tanner to pass. He shot her a subdued smile and closed the door to follow.

She rushed around the desk to throw the lock, resting against the solid wood. Yes, she promised to be open for office hours, but she needed a minute to pull herself together. Her knees felt like jelly and her hands wouldn't stop shaking. She blotted sweat from her upper lip and temples as she dropped into the nearest chair.

Rolling her wrist, she thought today's outburst was a thousand times worse than the night he'd struck her. Today he'd been sober.

After a few deep breaths, her pulse slowed down and she made her way back to her side of the desk to put the phone to rights. It was hard to believe

Tanner would make such a scene where anyone could catch him in the act.

He'd been in this area and in property development long enough to know the historical society would've looked closely at the site where he planned to build. No matter what he believed, she didn't think there was any way his plan would have gone through. Someone would have raised a fuss at one of the zoning meetings.

The details and records she'd unearthed about early life on that bend in the Cooper River weren't necessarily common knowledge or tourist hotspots, but the church and family enterprise in that particular location were important to the overall picture of early life and growth in the area. He could blame her all he wanted, but if he'd listened, he might have saved his money.

As the new property owner he could salvage his investment, if he had any interest in promoting community engagement and pride. But she'd learned the hard way that Tanner wasn't the type to be genuinely interested in civic outreach and generosity.

She had no idea how much time she'd been sitting there when a knock on the closed door startled her out of her reverie. She stood, grateful her knees felt normal again, and went to the door. Pausing, she coached herself that it couldn't be Tanner. Logan wouldn't have allowed him back inside.

She opened the door to a student and invited her in. Dismissing the concerned query, she threw herself into the work she loved. Allison was fully aware when Logan passed by the open door and truly grateful that he didn't interrupt to check on her. It would only have raised more questions she wasn't ready to answer, especially not in front of a student.

And she had several questions of her own, starting with how he'd dealt with Tanner. She wouldn't begrudge him any solution or tactic, as long as her ex got the message and left her alone.

CHAPTER 9

LOGAN STRUGGLED to keep his focus for the afternoon session. He'd committed to the Marines to teach this class over the summer term and he would fulfill it to the best of his ability. But as he stood at the window, checking the parking lot again for any sign of Tanner's return, he was glad the task wasn't more demanding of his time or his attention.

The bastard was dangerous and escalating. There's no telling what he might've done to Allison in the office if Logan hadn't walked by. He'd been on his way to her office for the sole purpose of stealing a quick kiss and to make plans for dinner. And what would happen *after* dinner.

He hadn't been pleased to find her ex harassing her again. Why wouldn't the man leave her alone? It made no sense. Her report was basically public record now. He'd be better off looking for a new buyer for the land than trying to force through a development that would be stalled indefinitely.

Once Tanner had left the school premises, Logan stopped by the campus security office to report Tanner's visit. He wanted as many eyes as possible on the lookout, ready to step in and keep the jerk away from Allison.

When that was handled, he called Jenna. He'd given his account of their tense conversation before his intervention and together they talked through it, trying to make sense of Tanner's aggressive actions. At the moment all they knew was that too many pieces were missing.

Still, Tanner's unpleasant visit hadn't muted Logan's anticipation over what might be in store tonight. Those hot kisses kept running through his mind, the feel of her sweet curves under his hands, and the eagerness for more that matched his own. Preferably to the nearest private bedroom if there was any justice left in the world.

He'd had all night to think it over and he'd come to the conclusion that the intense chemistry between them was too rare to ignore or shove under the rock of friendship. In his opinion, that friendship and the longstanding trust only enhanced the sizzling physical spark.

Finally, his class ended and he was alone in the classroom. Logan called Jenna first, praying she'd found an explanation or something tangible for him to pursue. Then he could go and get things moving in the right direction with Allison. Assuming she agreed with him.

"I've got some bad news for you," Jenna said.

"Lay it on me," he said.

"Wait. That sounds like a good mood," Jenna observed. "You told me you didn't beat on him."

"I didn't lay a hand on him." Any goodness in his mood or his heart was tied to what he hoped would be an unforgettable evening with Allison. "Maybe I just love being back in Charleston."

"Right." She dragged out the word. "My guess is you found someone to help you navigate these big life changes. I bet she's a tall blonde with a beach volleyball build who rocks a bikini."

Logan's mind filled with a vision of Allison's gorgeous curves filling out a skimpy hot-pink bikini and was instantly hard. Whoops, definitely not a vision to dwell on here at work, but something to look forward to over the weekend.

"I'm not into tall women. I'm only five-five myself."

Jenna cackled. "I know better."

Logan felt a smile cross his face. "Oh really how?"

"Cameras, my friend. I've seen you plenty on surveillance already. Plus there's the little matter of your military record," she added. "They hire me to get all the details and dirt where most people don't even know it exists."

"You're a little scary," he admitted. "Did you find any dirt on Tanner?

"The man has connections all over the place, not just in Charleston. And he's in debt up to his eyeballs. I'm tracking down the full list of who he owes, but believe me when I say the only money in his bank account right now looks dirty."

Given what he'd seen of Tanner's selfishness, it was no surprise that the man might have unsavory investors in his pocket or made shady deals along the way. Granted, Logan was biased and protective of Allison, but something was off about how Tanner was fixated on her.

"Let me know when you figure out what's going on with the money," Logan said. "Do you have any indication he's trying to buy off city councils or someone on the zoning board?"

"Indications, but no proof," Jenna said. "I'm unraveling this mess as fast as I can. If I find anything alarming I'll notify the police and then you. In that order."

"As long as the delay doesn't put Allison in jeopardy," Logan agreed.

"I've been at this longer than you," Jenna reminded him. "I know the priorities."

"Thanks." He wasn't trying to be an ass about this. He and Jenna were on their way to becoming a great team. They just needed a few more cases to build up the trust. "I appreciate always having good intel."

Once he made a commitment, he would go to bat for that mission or a client. That was just how he was made. But Allison was special. Her safety wasn't just important, it was paramount to his peace of mind.

A chill slammed through him when he thought about what might've happened to Allison, who she could've turned to, if the Corps hadn't assigned him here this summer. Or if he hadn't signed with the Guardian Agency.

Deliberately looking away from that dark abyss of what ifs, he asked Jenna to send him a list of Tanner's assets and personal associates.

"I can do that. What are you thinking?" she asked.

"I'm not planning anything petty or juvenile. I won't even stalk him," he promised. Her GPS reports covered that. "I'd like to get a feel of where he might be spending his time," he explained.

Logan might do a little drive-by reconnaissance here or there, but more than that, he wanted to know where Tanner *should* be throughout the day. The jerk seemed to always pop up to give Allison grief.

No, Charleston wasn't nearly as crowded or as congested as other major cities but still it bothered him that Tanner always managed to be close. Yes, a person could drive across town in thirty minutes, barring a traffic accident or torrential rain, but if he was tracking her somehow, they needed to know it now.

LATE IN THE AFTERNOON, Allison received a text from Logan that he'd meet her at her office after classes. She was pretty sure his schedule didn't match hers at all, but she appreciated his determination to keep Tanner from surprising her again. He knocked on her open office door and the warm smile lit a fire of desire deep in her belly.

"You all right?" he asked, leaning against the door jamb.

She would be once she had a chance to kiss him again. His eyes were full of concern, but the rest of him was nothing but temptation. "I am now. Can you come in and close the door?"

"No." His mouth kicked up at one corner in a sexy smirk. "The next time I'm alone with you, I want a bed within easy reach."

She gasped.

His brow furrowed. "Unless you don't feel the same."

"Of course I do." Heat flooded her face and images of him taking her right here on the desk nearly caused her knees to buckle. In a hurry now, she gathered her things. "Let's, um, just go."

At his low laughter, she assumed her need for him was clear as day as they walked out to the parking lot. He walked her right to the car. "Your place or mine?" he asked.

Everything inside her went fluttery. He was as excited to pick up where they'd left off as she was. "Mine. I'll fix dinner."

"All right." He smoothed a wisp of her hair behind her ear. "Eventually we'll be hungry."

The deep rumble of his voice sent a shiver of anticipation over her skin. The short drive would feel like an eternity. If only it was appropriate for her to throw herself at him right here, but making out in the parking lot was a kid thing to do. They were adults and should probably set a better example.

He opened her car door and she smiled, sinking into the driver's seat. "Want a lift to your truck?"

"No, thanks. Safer for both of us if I walk." His gaze had dropped to her mouth.

She licked her lips.

"Stop." His voice was strained. "You don't want us to get caught steaming up the windows."

She laughed. "In the summertime a purely platonic conversation could do that."

He arched an eyebrow and donned his sunglasses. "I'm not taking that chance."

Somehow she managed not to grab him by the shirtfront and drag him into the car with her. "See you at my place."

"Count on it," he said.

Allison watched him cross the parking lot to his truck, admiring his long legs and firm backside. It was pure bliss to watch Logan move. Always had been. Even when she refused to see him as more than a friend. She couldn't recall him suffering an awkward age from the time they'd met. He had an innate confidence and athletic grace that was stronger than ever now that he'd matured.

Last night's kiss had been worth the risk and it

was a thrill to be on the receiving end of those long, steamy looks and flirty comments.

On a sigh, she pulled out of her parking space, circling around to wait for him. A silly move since he knew his way to her condo, but she just didn't want to let him out of her sight.

His head down, he appeared to be lost in thought as he approached his vehicle and lifted the key fob to unlock the door. She saw another man behind him and her mind immediately registered danger.

The man was about the same height as Logan and he wore a loose, dark blue T-shirt with a logo for another local college over gray athletic shorts. She didn't see an obvious weapon, but something just didn't feel right. He was too intent on Logan.

It all seemed to happen at once. Logan reached for the door handle at the same time the man quickened his steps, an arm raised.

He was holding a gun! Allison threw her car into Park and shouted Logan's name as she pressed on the car horn.

Logan jerked at the sound and the blaring disruption threw off the shooter's aim. The truck window shattered from the bullet, missing Logan.

She honked the horn again, trying to bring more attention as the man closed in on Logan. Where was campus security? This time of year everyone was on a skeleton crew at the college, but those on duty would show up. They had to.

She scrambled for her cell phone and dialed 9-1-1, hands shaking with fear that Logan would be injured. At last the operator picked up and Allison gave a description of the attacker and her location.

From her vantage point it looked as though Logan had the upper hand. Then the man twisted and Logan went down hard, his head bouncing on the asphalt. She started to climb out of her car, only to be stopped by the responding campus security team. Their presence was enough to send the attacker running and two security officers gave chase.

Unable to stand by, she exited her car despite the protests and hurried to Logan's side. Her heart hammered and she could barely hear anything over the blood thundering through her veins. Landing on her knees, she cradled his head between her hands. "Don't move." There was blood on the pavement and she feared the worst.

Oh, this was all her fault. Had to be. Who else would take a swipe at him like this except for Tanner?

"Talk to me," she pleaded. Logan's eyelids fluttered and he squinted up at her. "Can you move your fingers and toes?" This could *not* be happening. She couldn't lose him just when they'd found something even more wonderful than their friendship.

"Allison?"

She gulped in a breath. "I'm so sorry." She brushed a smudge of dirt from his face. Then a tear that rolled off her cheek and fell on his. "Please talk to me, Logan." Sirens were screaming closer. "Help is on the way."

It wasn't at all fair for life to bring him through a military career in one piece and then deal him a blow like this. Because of her. Guilt pressed in on her from all sides and red hazed her vision. When she saw Tanner again, she'd knock him on his ass.

Logan shifted, attempting to sit up. "No stay where you are." She pressed a hand to his shoulder. "You might have a concussion, or worse."

"I've had both," Logan said, reaching back to feel his scalp. "Head wounds bleed and look worse than they are. You know that."

"Yes but—"

"You saved me from something far worse. Good move, laying on the horn. Thank you." He moved her hand to his lips and kissed her fingers.

She let him sit up, but only to get a better look at the wound on his head. "I'm sorry about your truck and all the rest." Please let him be right about the minor injuries. "My mess shouldn't be yours."

"Stop apologizing to me," he said, his voice bordering on harsh. "You didn't do this." He caught her hands, and they both stared down and the dirt and blood on his palms. "It hurts," he admitted. "But it's not serious."

"I'll wait for the paramedics to weigh in." She sniffed back more tears. He didn't need her wallowing on top of everything else. "You might need stitches." She looked around, hoping to see some sign that they'd caught the attacker.

"Did you get a good look at him?" Logan asked, clearly on the same page as she was.

"Yes." She gave a nod and sat back, relieved he was feeling well enough to ask questions.

"You don't need to fuss over me," he said as he slowly gained his feet.

"Too bad." She slid an arm around his waist. "I'm going to keep it up a while."

He opened his truck door and reached into the space behind the driver's seat, pulling out a bottle of water. He opened it, took a drink and then poured more water over her hands to wash away his blood. "There that's better," he said.

"Turn around and let me do the same for your head. It'll keep me busy until the paramedics can take over," she added when he started to protest.

"Fine." He walked over and dropped the truck's

tailgate so he could sit down, making the task easier for her.

He shivered a little when the water dripped down his back. She figured the button-down shirt he wore was a loss anyway, torn at the sleeve and stained with dirt and blood. When he got home he would surely want to shower off the entire incident. It was ridiculous and selfish that she hoped he'd invite her to help with that particular task, but still she imagined it, trying to replace the ugliness and fear with happier thoughts.

"Are you willing to see how deep it is?" he asked, bursting her bubble.

"No." She chewed on her lip. "Do you need me to do it?"

"Nah. I've survived worse." He smiled, his eyes warm and comforting.

"Stop being nice." Her voice trembled, shaming her. "This was horrible. You could've died and I—" She caught herself before she told him she loved him. Not best friend love, but falling in love. One hot series of kisses didn't justify that kind of declaration, even if it was true.

All they knew right now was that they wanted to see where this new facet of their relationship might lead.

"You what?" he prompted.

"I'm a mess," she said, sagging against the tailgate.

The paramedics had arrived and were being directed toward Logan. "Tanner mentioned resources. Do you think he did this?" He finished under his breath as authorities surrounded them.

She gave him a quick nod and watched the scowl take shape before she was guided a few paces away to give her statement about the incident to campus security and the police officers who had arrived. Carefully, she gave the details fact by fact and was dismayed to hear the attacker had eluded them.

When the police asked if she knew anyone who might want to hurt Logan, she claimed she didn't know. Something about the hard look on Logan's face made her want to confer with him before volunteering any more information about Tanner's possible involvement. She knew how to reach the authorities if she wanted to add something to her statement later.

Released from her conversation, she returned to Logan's side in time to catch the last of the paramedic's instructions. "You aren't showing immediate signs of a concussion, but unless you have somebody to keep an eye on you tonight, I recommend going to the hospital to be sure."

"He has someone," she said. She was not going to be parted from him tonight for any reason.

"Lucky guy." The paramedic smiled and handed her a piece of paper. "As I said, it shouldn't be a problem, but this is what to watch for."

"Thank you." She folded the paper in half and then peeked at the clean white bandage at the base of his skull. "I'm glad you're okay."

"Me too," he agreed, gifting her with a soft smile. "Any chance I can beg a ride? The police want some time with my truck for evidence."

She laced her fingers through his. "Your place or mine?"

"Mine," he said with quiet certainty. "It doesn't have all the amenities of your place, but then again, my name isn't on any record with that address."

The implication that he thought Tanner was watching her house gave her chills, but there were too many people around to speak freely. "We could just tell them our theory now," she said as they walked to her car.

"Not yet." Logan's voice was hard. He waited to speak again until they were both closed into her car and pulling away. "If we point the police at him too soon nothing will stick. He might even leave town. I want him to face the consequences for the trouble he's caused you."

"I want that too."

He reached over and squeezed her hand. "Can

you trust me on this for another day or two at most?"

"I've trusted you forever," she said.

She believed in Logan's skills, in the support of his new affiliation with the bodyguard agency. But Tanner's earlier words about resources echoed in her head.

CHAPTER 10

SHE PARKED in his driveway and dutifully ignored the wince of pain as he walked gingerly to the front door. It wasn't fair that he'd been attacked and she was eager to do all she could to make up for it. When they were inside and Logan had set the deadbolts, she lifted his hand to her lips. "I'm so sorry."

"Please stop apologizing." He brought her in for a hug, and she was careful not to cling too tightly. "It wasn't your fault."

She cleared her throat, willing to try and see it his way. "Why don't you grab a shower and I'll order something for dinner."

"I won't argue with that," he said. "Can you help me with this shirt?"

"No." She shook her head. "I want you too much and you're compromised."

He cocked an eyebrow. "Is this some kind of payback for last night?"

She liked the spark in his eyes, the heat building there. "Maybe? Let's see how you're feeling after dinner."

But after dinner, he was groggy and she tucked him into the bed, promising him there would be plenty of time for this explosive attraction when he felt better. At his insistence, she crawled under the covers with him, but guilt kept her awake.

Guilt and fear that something else would happen and steal him from her before they had a chance.

The next day he woke her with soft kisses and breakfast in bed before they had to be at the school. "Do you still want more than kisses?" he asked.

She nodded, bewildered that they were here in this limbo.

"Good. When classes are over, we're going straight to your place," he stated, a wicked gleam in his eyes. "I don't care what tries to stop us."

"Why my place?"

"Because it's your home. This place is just a temporary landing spot."

She stewed on that all day long, wondering exactly what he meant. It felt significant enough that her pulse would accelerate and her lips would tingle.

By the time he met her at her office at the end of the day, she was a ball of bone-deep longing.

He held her hand on the drive over, kissed her for several minutes after she parked in her space in front of her building. And this time when they reached her door, she got him inside before she let him kiss her again.

She dropped her keys and computer bag right there at the door, along with her purse. Unbuttoning his shirt, she slid her hands up and over that hard, sculpted chest. "You're glorious," she said, pressing a kiss over his heart. She would've kicked off her shoes, but he picked her up and she wrapped herself around him.

"I need you," she said against his mouth. Everything. All of him. She tunneled her hands through his thick hair, savoring every sensation.

His hands tightened on her hips and he pulled her right up against his erection. She moaned. He made a sound deep in his throat and walked to the couch, laying her down. For a long moment he just stared, looking almost shell-shocked.

She knew just how he felt.

He removed her shoes and his big hands glided up and over her legs, under her skirt. She'd had to wear most of the same outfit as the day before, pairing yesterday's skirt with one of his button-down shirts over a camisole. Her body quivered as he neared the apex of her thighs, his touch barely there as he traced the lace edge of her panties.

She surged up, desperate for more of his drugging kisses. They were really doing this. It felt so perfect already. She shoved his open shirt off of his shoulders and just indulged in a long look. A light dusting of hair highlighted his chest, and below his navel the hair was darker, arrowing straight down. A path she couldn't wait to follow. "God, you're hot."

His mouth dropped open and then he laughed. She was blushing but it didn't matter, couldn't possibly be noticeable with the fever he stirred all through her system. He was amazing.

She arched into his palms as he cupped her breasts. Then his mouth covered each nipple in turn and he worked her with lips and teeth until she was on the edge of a climax. She wriggled out of her skirt and started on his fly.

"The bed..." His voice trailed off as she wrapped her hand around his erection.

"Too far away. Here, Logan. I'm begging you."

His mouth tilted into a grin. "You will be."

He kissed a path down her body and dragged her panties out of the way, spreading her legs to accommodate his broad shoulders. She was fully exposed to him and had never felt so safe. When he pressed his mouth to her inner thigh his five o'clock shadow brushed her core and she whimpered.

"Talk to me," he crooned against her sensitive flesh. "Tell me what you need."

Heat climbed into her cheeks. She'd never done much talking during sex. But this wasn't random, it was Logan. She'd always been able to tell him anything.

Anything. Longing arced through her as he breathed against her center. "You'll do the same?"

"Mm-hmm." He lapped at her slick folds, once, then withdrew. "I need to make you come."

"I need that too," she confessed. She was already panting.

"How do you want it?" He was teasing her with light touches and soft breaths against the bundle of nerves that needed so much more, but she would've sworn she'd felt those touches on her heart. "Can't hear you, baby."

"Your mouth." Was she really saying this stuff? "Please, Logan." If he made her get any more specific she might combust before she could climax.

He was either too enthralled to keep up the talking game, or he understood her limits. His mouth covered her, his tongue strumming her with a firm and tantalizing pressure as he discovered what she enjoyed most. He'd build her up, carry her to the edge and back off just enough that he could start again. The sweetest torture, until she was begging him to let the pleasure sweep her away.

The first orgasm rocketed through her, his name on her lips. She couldn't wait to get her mouth on him, but he stripped away his slacks and moved her pliant body until she was straddling his legs.

"Allison, look at me."

Floating on that sensual wave, it was worth the effort to see that intensity, that need aimed at her. Slowly he drew her hips closer to his erection. As she watched him apply the condom, she traced circles over his beautiful torso. She rested a hand over his heart and everything inside her settled at that rapid hammering in his chest. He was feeling it too. The rush and the thrill riding alongside, the difference in this moment.

Cradling his face, she laid her mouth on his. With slow, deep kisses, she glided up and over his shaft, taking him inside inch by inch.

His body tensed, but he didn't rush her. She felt stretched and whole, in the most delicious way. Being joined to him suffused her, like watching the sun come over the ocean. She found her rhythm in a slow rise and fall as he fondled her breasts. She braced her hands on his shoulders changing the angle. He groaned. "How can I make it better, Logan?"

"Come closer."

She obliged and he lifted her breasts to his mouth, nuzzling and sucking on her tight nipples. Her rhythm slipped, but he caught her. He touched his thumb to her clit and she bucked, clenching around him until he groaned. "Faster, Allison. I'm begging you."

She matched the pace he set, hanging on to those strong shoulders. The next orgasm took her by surprise and she shuddered, her legs quivering as he thrust into her, finding his own release.

He pulled her close, feathering soft kisses along her collarbone, up to her ear. "You're beautiful." After a few minutes of boneless bliss, he got up to deal with the condom and then returned and to her fascination, he plucked her up and carried her back to her bedroom.

Under the covers, she rested in his embrace while the echoes of the most amazing and sensual experience of her life lulled her to sleep.

CHAPTER 11

EVERY MINUTE that Logan was away from Allison felt as if he was dangling her out as bait. It wasn't the case at all, but he couldn't shake the sensation that she was in danger whenever she was out of his sight.

The last few days had been a strange mix of heaven and hell. Sweet kisses in the morning, nights full of creative, passionate lovemaking offset by days full of apprehension over what Tanner might try next.

He was having sex with his best friend and it was phenomenal. Life altering and he never wanted to go back to a time without her.

What he thought he knew about Allison and what he was learning was shaping up into something unexpectedly beautiful. Deeper and more meaningful than he'd ever expected from their friendship.

And almost too bright to look at directly. He wasn't sure he could be what she needed. At least not outside of the bedroom. But he was consumed with a desire to try.

The first step was making sure she was safe.

Logan was convinced that going quiet didn't mean her ex had given up on his goal to develop that land. Jenna had tracked Tanner's banking activity and the BMW, but nothing was moving in unexpected ways. She had a line on his other two vehicles now, but they remained at his home address.

The man who'd attacked him in the parking lot still hadn't been located and Logan assumed he'd been shuffled out of the city on Tanner's dime. Between classes, he strolled down to Allison's lecture hall and was relieved to find that all was well. He still hadn't told her about his visit with campus security, not wanting to stress her out. They were all actively watching for Tanner or anyone else who didn't belong on campus.

When he returned to his own classroom, empty for the day, he called Jenna. "Tell me we have something."

"You have perfect timing," she said. "We assumed Tanner would lose millions if he can't build on that site and we're right. But I also peeled back the layers on one of his investors. The construction would

launder a significant chunk of money for an orga-
nized crime group based in the Caribbean."

"Seriously?"

"Yes. But it all hinges on construction actually
happening. Tanner will either be bankrupt or dead
soon if he can't build on that land."

"But Allison's reports have been submitted. She
won't retract them. Too many people know what she
found."

"Which is probably why he's spent the last
seventy-two hours searching for experts to contradict her."

That just pissed him off. "She *is* the authority on
this stuff, Jenna. I doubt there's an expert in this area
who *can or would* contradict her."

"Easy, tiger. I'm on your side," Jenna reminded
him. "Per my usual, I've done my due diligence on
our not-officially-a-client as well as her ugly ex. All
the players get the full treatment when I'm on a
case."

He did his best to unclench his jaw. "Good."
Logan would find her diligence far more reassuring
on a normal case. He wasn't at all comfortable with
Jenna knowing how much personal time he was
spending with Allison.

"And you're right about your girl being the top
authority," Jenna continued. "But Tanner only has to

convince the *right* people to get his plans approved and pushed through," she finished.

That was true enough. And frustrating. Allison would be miserable if Tanner won and destroyed a valuable piece of local history. If the man was still in town with money in the bank, he still had some hope that he could succeed.

Logan paced up and down the empty hallway, his hand tight on the phone. Given a choice he would glue himself to her hip until Tanner got himself killed. It didn't matter that Jenna had vetted all of her students, and none of them showed any sign of wanting to hurt their professor. If she wasn't beside him he couldn't protect her and that wasn't going to work for him long term.

"Give me something I can use to make Tanner crack," he said.

"Something besides your fists?"

"Come on, Jenna. Work with me. I'm missing something important."

She sighed. "You're not. I wish I had the answers, believe me." He heard the soft rattle of the keyboard as she entered or searched or whatever she was up to. "He's got influence and still has enough money in his account to buy off key people, if necessary. Maybe he's resigned to that course and will leave her alone now."

That wasn't enough of a guarantee for Logan. "That still doesn't explain the direct attack on me." Or the immediate absence of trouble in the days since. He couldn't explain it, but he was sure Tanner was waiting to strike again. "It's not about jealousy. Allison told me that he ignored her pretty much from the moment they decided to be exclusive."

"Proof that many men are idiots," Jenna muttered.

Logan couldn't argue with that. "He doesn't act like a guy obsessed or in love. This is about him. About saving his own ass, but it isn't adding up." If he could buy approval for his project, why hassle Allison at all?

"Then I guess we'll both keep digging until something breaks," Jenna said.

As long as Allison wasn't the one in pieces when it was over. "I'll ask Allison what she knows about the people he'd be trying to bribe." The alarm he'd set to alert him to the end of her class went off. "Gotta go," he said, ending the call.

He headed toward the lecture hall and watched her students exit, acknowledging those who made eye contact as he strode by. It unnerved him to see so many people and no sign of her. There were at least a hundred students enrolled for this session, far too many people for her to know every face.

A short scream sounded from the inside the lecture hall. It could be anyone, but he shoved through the sea of bodies, carving a path. His heart stuttered when he heard the shout for help. That was definitely Allison.

He grabbed a burly kid who'd started to turn back. "Call security."

"What can we do?" another young man asked.

A small crowd had gathered and they were all looking to him for directions. "Get people on every exit from that room," he ordered. "No one gets out. And don't let anyone in until I give the all clear."

The students scattered and he burst into the hall and seeing what he was up against, felt that calm he'd relied on during military operations fall over him. Sound faded, secondary to the scene playing out in front of him. Allison was fighting against a lean young man who could have passed as a student but was obviously a stranger.

"Stop!" Logan shouted. He was too far away. Instinctively, he reached for a sidearm, but he was a civilian now and he didn't keep a gun on his hip anymore.

The man had been grappling with her, but now he stopped and swiveled and from one heartbeat to the next, he had a knife pressed to Allison's throat. "Stay back," he warned.

"No chance," Logan said. "Drop the knife and I'll let you walk out of here."

The man only laughed. Allison struggled and he knew she would try to create an opening. He also trusted her to make the most of it when it happened.

To an outsider it surely appeared that the odds were stacked against Logan. He was at the top of the auditorium and Allison and her assailant were near the central desk. But unless the man had an accomplice or a getaway car waiting in the hallway behind the auditorium, there was no chance he was getting out of here with the woman Logan loved. The woman he'd die for.

"What's your name?" He advanced, one slow step after another.

"John Doe," the kid replied.

"Let her go, John."

"Stop moving."

Logan froze and held up his hands. "Come on. Work with me."

"Can't. Sorry, pal. You don't get to be a hero today."

It probably looked that way to the guy with the knife. "How do you know Professor Weaver, John?"

"I don't." His shoulders rocked as if holding Allison was making him cramp up. "They sent a picture. Wired money."

So the kid had been hired to do this. That kind of thing had Tanner's fingerprints all over it. But was the goal to frighten, kidnap, or kill her? "Lower the knife and walk away."

"Can't." He took a step toward the door, dragging Allison with him. "Gave my word."

Logan advanced again, slow and steady, as John Doe tried to retreat with his prize.

"I said stay back!"

Allison hissed as the blade pressed against the delicate skin under her chin.

Logan paused. He'd put his lips on that very spot in the shower this morning. And damn it, he vowed that he'd kiss her there again before she fell asleep in his arms tonight.

He met her gaze. She was clearly uncomfortable and scared, but her eyes were dry. She wasn't going to break. "So you're not a student." Logan took another step. "She never gave you a bad grade or anything like that?"

"No, man. It's just a job. Let me do it." The last words had a bit of a whine in them.

"Why don't we renegotiate."

"What do you mean?"

"Whatever you got paid, I can double it," Logan said. "No one needs to get hurt today."

"Can't. My rep matters. If I renege it's the end of my career."

"Seems like you need another line of work, John." Logan moved forward. So close, but not yet close enough to attack.

Allison had been shaking, tripping over her feet, doing everything possible to make it difficult for John Doe to haul her out of this auditorium. His woman was smart and brave. Her fingers curled around John's wrist. "What do you want from me?"

"Just cooperate," John replied.

Logan took two more steps, praying the students who'd offered to help had all of the exits covered by now. The only good news was that he was up against a knife rather than a gun. The lethal aspect was the same, but the chance of a knife randomly going off and injuring an innocent bystander was much lower.

He was close enough to calculate angles and potential risk of injury for Allison and himself. "You were hired to kill her?"

The question sent Allison into a panic. She cried out and fought harder to get free of John's grip.

The man yanked her hard, and a line of blood trickled down her neck.

Fury blazed white hot through Logan and he barely kept himself in check. If he acted too early, he'd lose any advantage and Allison could be seriously wounded. Not while he still had breath and a pulse.

"The exits are blocked," Logan said. "All of them. Your best bet is to deal with me. Right here. Offer expires in thirty seconds."

"Sorry, man. I took a job and I have to follow through whether I like it or not."

"He asked for the research first," Allison blurted out. "All the copies."

Tanner was definitely behind this. Suddenly the attempt on his life a few days ago made sense. With Logan out of the way, Tanner had a clear path to kidnap or kill Allison and destroy or alter any hard copies of her research. Then he only had to get rid of the original record she'd filed.

John Doe swore and shuffled her back toward the big desk to grab her computer bag. Logan capital-ized on the distraction, storming down the last of the stairs. John didn't make it to the door. Off balance, having to choose between the briefcase or the woman, he couldn't defend himself against Logan's assault.

He would apologize later for shoving Allison to the floor. His priority was making sure this guy answered some serious questions, before they locked him up. With two quick motions, he knocked the knife away and dislocated the man's shoulder. He landed a hard kick to John's knee and when he was down, held him there, ignoring the groans of pain.

"Tell me who hired you and I can make this easier for you," Logan demanded.

One of the doors opened at the top of the auditorium. "Campus security is on the way," the young man guarding the door called out.

"Good." Logan gave John Doe a hard shake. "Tell me."

"Man, I was hired to kill her. How easy can you make it?"

Hearing Allison's shocked gasp, he regretted having this conversation in front of her. "You might be surprised," Logan muttered. "I know a couple of good attorneys." He would bet his retirement this kid had never killed anyone and didn't plan to actually kill her.

He sat back, letting the kid get a full breath. "What was your plan? Who wanted her dead?"

"I don't know. N-no names," he stammered. "I swear I wasn't going to hurt her." He leaned around Logan. "I wasn't gonna hurt you."

"But you took the contract to kill her?"

"Along with her research." Tears leaked from the corners of his eyes. "I didn't think anybody would find out if I didn't, y'know, go through with it. I swear."

Logan shook his head. "Who wouldn't have found out?"

He groaned. "Tanner Aultman. A bouncer from that club he owns handled the deal. Said his boss needed an ex out of the way. You dated him, right?"

"Right," Allison murmured.

Logan got in John Doe's face. "He told you to kill her?"

"Yeah," he admitted reluctantly.

"And you agreed?" Allison sounded more offended than frightened now. "This is obscene."

"The money was obscene," John Doe said. "I lost my job and I lost a scholarship and I swear I just need the money. I wasn't going to hurt you."

There was a commotion as the security team took over. Logan relinquished his prisoner and gathered Allison close, rubbing her back. "The police will take it from here. I won't let Tanner get out of this," he promised her.

She wrapped her arms tightly around his waist. "Thank you for being here. For saving me."

"I don't ever want to be anywhere else," he said. "But I'm pretty sure you would've saved yourself."

"I don't know." She leaned back, tunneling her hands through her hair. "Tanner would've killed me to suppress or alter my research."

He tipped her chin up, relieved that the mark on

her neck was only a small scratch. "Best we can figure right now, it's your life or his."

"And his is the only life that matters," she said, temper flashing in her eyes.

"Agreed."

For now, he had all the confirmation he needed that Tanner wouldn't quit. Allison would never be safe while her ex believed he could hire people to hunt her down. It was high time Logan put the bastard out of business.

CHAPTER 12

"Do you need anything, Professor Weaver?"

Allison looked up into the face of one of the young men who'd helped Logan keep John Doe in the auditorium. For the life of her, she couldn't put a name to his face. "I'm fine."

His cocked his head, clearly skeptical. "You look a little shaky." He draped a blanket over her shoulders. Did anything say 'victim' more than that particular gesture?

"It'll pass." It was all the assurance she could offer. They'd nudged her into a chair in the front row, but her heart continued to race. She only felt steady when Logan was within reach. No surprise there. He'd been her one solid constant from the days when her biggest problem in life was a bully on the playground.

She looked to him now and felt her breathing even out while he spoke with the police.

The paramedics had cleaned the small nick under her chin. It had stopped bleeding but when she touched it, her fingers came away sticky from whatever they'd used. She wanted to wash it off, to scrub away any trace of the man who'd tried to kidnap her.

I wasn't going to hurt you. Those words echoed in her head. Maybe this John Doe had planned to let her go, but what about the next one? Her fingers curled around the arm of the seat and she had to focus on her breathing or the scream building in her lungs would break free.

Then Logan was beside her, his long fingers covering hers, lending warmth. "How are you holding up?"

"Not as well as I'd like." She scooped her hair back from her face. "Can we go?"

He nodded. "We can. Just as soon as we finish giving our statements." His gaze moved over the scene.

The John Doe with the knife had been taken away, but too many uniformed officials and students milled about. She felt as if everyone was staring at her, though they really weren't. At last the city police and campus security teams were done with her for the moment. She and Logan were asked to cooperate and be available for more interviews as necessary.

"Will you drive?" Her hand shook as she handed him her keys. "Please?"

"Absolutely." He pulled her to her feet and his fingers were gentle as he lifted her chin to examine the wound on her neck. His hazel eyes turned stormy.

"It's minor," she said.

"Still left a mark." His gaze met hers. "On more than your skin, I think."

Leave it to Logan to see right through her. "Thank you again. I don't know what I would've done without you."

"You'd have thought of something." When she was on her feet, he pulled her tight against his body. "You're the bravest woman I know," he whispered into her hair.

She looked around as they walked out. They'd discussed the inherent hazard of her taking on a class of this size, in this room, without him or some other security personnel inside. She regretted being stubborn about it. He might well have been hurt trying to protect her from an attack he could've prevented.

"You were right." She flicked a hand at the auditorium behind them. "I never should have tried to have this class alone."

"Don't do that," he scolded softly. "You can't let this incident color everything. There's risk every time we open a door and step outside."

It was true, but she also knew it would be a long while before she would feel comfortable in this room or any other if she didn't know every face.

"Maybe I should take that sabbatical Tanner was harping about."

Logan frowned. "When did he suggest that?"

"Last year. Just before we broke up actually. I was spending a great deal of time on the research and he felt neglected."

"Or, in light of what he's put you through, maybe he felt threatened."

She stared at Logan, momentarily stunned. "You think he wanted to bury my research back then?"

"Bury it, stop it. Anything to get his project off the ground. He owes some impatient, ruthless people a lot of money."

"We attended countless functions. He would go on and on about concepts and proposals, but he never mentioned wanting to develop in the area where I was researching."

"Regardless, it adds up."

"What now, Logan?"

"The kid is cooperating with the police. Even if Tanner didn't hire him directly, he won't slip through this unscathed. The police will just need time to follow the leads and gather enough evidence against Tanner."

"So it's over?" she wondered when they reached her car.

Where did that leave the two of them? Surely he didn't plan to just go back to being good friends, preferably with excellent benefits.

His gaze was scanning the parking lot even as he opened the door for her. "I'd like to say this is all behind us, but until Tanner is in custody, I don't trust the man as far as I can throw him. Can you put up with me hovering for a little while longer?"

Hovering? Good grief. She was far more worried he'd wake up one morning and realize she was too clingy. "You're my best friend," she began. "And so much more." She kissed him and then dropped into the seat. "I'm happy to have you close for as long as it suits you."

There, that sounded mature and sensible. So why did the words feel inadequate?

He gave her a long study and then put his sunglasses over his eyes and went to the driver's side. He started the car, but didn't put it into gear.

Warm air blasted across her face for a second before the air conditioning kicked in.

Finally, he reached over and gently turned her to face him. "I'm not in any hurry to move on, Allison. Crisis or not." Then he brushed his lips across hers.

Heat shimmered through her system, dulling those sharp edges that lingered after the attack. She relaxed as they crossed the river, headed for her place tonight.

Logan spoiled her, taking care of everything so all she had to do was shower and rest. He urged her to cancel her classes for the rest of the week, but work was the easier solution. Other than Logan himself, work was the best possible distraction.

Better to focus on grading papers and lecture notes than think about Tanner's deadly desperation. Or how in love she was with Logan.

He'd ordered dinner delivered from one of her favorite restaurants and opened a bottle of wine to go with it. Though he chatted with her, a deep scowl kept falling over his face and she suspected he was making plans for Tanner's downfall.

It would bother her the rest of her days that she hadn't seen the depth of Tanner's ugliness from the start.

Logan's phone rang again, and this time he walked out on the balcony.

When her cell phone rang a moment later and Sadie's face filled the display, she had a pretty good idea who Logan was speaking with.

"You realize I can put two and two together?" Allison asked Sadie after exchanging 'hellos'.

"Of course, but why not chat and let the guys think they're clever?

Allison laughed in spite of everything. "How do you take times like this in stride? You can't possibly want Logan to drag Hank into this quagmire."

"As if I could keep him out of it," Sadie replied lightly. "And I've had years of practice my friend. You'll get there. Plus, I trust Hank to handle himself. Life has yet to throw my man a curveball he can't hit out of the park."

The comment reminded her too much of that first evening with Logan at the ball game.

"Should I assume your question means you're contemplating a future with Logan?"

He wasn't a teacher, he was a bodyguard and he was proving himself quite adept at the job. "Thinking about it and the reality of it are two different things. I don't want him to feel obligated to hang around just because he helped me out of a jam."

"You've been dealing with more than a jam, but that's a different issue." There was an irrepressible sparkle in Sadie's voice, evidence of a happy and contented woman. "How did you feel when he was in the Marines?" she queried at Allison's continued silence.

"Not much of anything," Allison hedged, watching Logan pace outside the glass doors. She had breathed easier with the arrival of every Christmas card. And she did keep an eye on the social media feeds of his friends, just to feel as if they were still in touch. "I mean, I was concerned for his safety, but we weren't close during those years."

"Do you want to be close now?"

"I don't want to lose him as a friend," Allison said. Sure they'd crossed the line to become lovers, but the friendship was invaluable to her. "I have no problem with his career choices..." Her voice trailed off as she tried to pin down her feelings.

"Then what is it?" Sadie pressed.

"I'm worried about holding him back." Logan was bigger than life to her. He made her feel safe and secure and gave her flagging confidence a boost. The way he handled himself in any crisis was admirable and more than a little mesmerizing. "At the end of the day I'm just a history professor and he's Superman."

"And I'm just a woman who pretends to be other people," Sadie said. "Hank is as real as they come and Logan strikes me the same. Whatever you're really worried about, try *talking* to him. You might get exactly what you've always wanted."

That was the real trouble with Logan coming home to stay, it shined a spotlight on the fact that she'd never truly wanted anyone but him. Sex was one thing but it would crush her if he chose to walk away.

"Okay, they're wrapping up," Sadie said. "Let's have Sunday brunch, all right? The spread here at the Ellington resort is amazing."

"I know it," Allison said, smiling. "It's a date, Sadie. Thank you."

She ended the call and Logan walked back inside, pocketing his phone as she set hers aside. "Is everything okay?" she asked.

"For tonight. Everyone tells me that Tanner is in the wind."

A chill prickled over her skin and she rubbed her arms.

"Don't worry." He crossed the room and cuddled her close. "Jenna's on it. He can't get out of town without leaving a trail she can find."

She snuggled closer. "With you here, I'm not worried at all." It was only a small fib and one she knew he could see right through. So she kissed him, distracting them both from a tough situation neither of them could control.

LOGAN WAS EDGY. He kept checking his phone, even though he had it set to an audible alert. Why hadn't Jenna found anything yet? It had been hours. Local law enforcement had Tanner's description and descriptions of his vehicles. The airport, train and bus stations had been notified, along with the marina where he kept a fishing boat. So far, no sightings.

It was inconceivable that the bastard would slip through the net. He'd promised Allison this would be over. He needed it to be over so he could have a serious talk without all these complications. He needed to tell her he loved her, that he wanted her in his life. Not just as a friend, but as his lover, his partner. He felt like he could do anything as long as he knew she was waiting for him to come back to a home they shared.

They were all assuming Tanner had been in town when his hired thug had attacked Allison at the school. What if the surprising lack of action was the head start Tanner needed to escape his enemies and the law?

"You can talk about it," Allison said. She was tucked into her oversized chair, grading essays because she was restless too.

He'd been trying to let her work in peace, but it was taking a crazy amount of energy to pretend everything was fine. "I don't mean to be twitchy." He tried a smile, and based on the consternation creasing her brow, he'd failed.

She set the papers aside and walked over, wrapping her arms around his waist. It felt so natural and right to slip his arms around her, to hold her close. He'd always cared about her, but in the past week their connection had reached a new depth. He wouldn't allow Tanner to destroy their happiness. She kissed him and the tenderness nearly leveled him. How had it only been a few days since they'd come together for the first time on this couch, a combustible mess of needs and desire?

"I want to take you out of here," he admitted, his fingers tracing the curve of her shoulder.

"It's a tempting thought." She snuggled closer, her hand resting lightly on his chest. "Hiding isn't my style any more than it's yours."

"No." He glanced at his phone, again. "If he's on the move, Jenna will find him. I'm surprised it's taking so long for her to pick up the trail."

"He has resources and a network of people who owe him favors," she said. On his chest, her fingers curled into her palm, her fist tough and hard. "I wish like hell I'd seen through that facade earlier."

He covered her hand, massaged gently until it loosened up. "It's going to be all right, I promise." He cupped the back of her head and kissed her. Pouring all of the words he was afraid to say aloud into the sweet, hot contact.

She drew him over to the couch and stretched out beneath him, her legs parting to cradle his hips. This was Allison, open and accepting and not even Tanner had wrecked that. She tugged at his shirt, gliding her palms over his back in a caress that only fueled his need for her.

"You have a thing for this couch," he murmured against her throat.

She chuckled. "If I do, you started it."

With her hands roaming, stirring up pleasure and excitement, he couldn't focus on conversation. Tanner became a distant threat. They were safe in her condo. The police were on alert, Jenna was monitoring every available camera and Hank was stationed nearby.

He gave himself over to the beauty and joy of the woman in his arms, the woman he'd fallen in love with despite his best efforts.

CHAPTER 13

SATED from Logan's remarkable stamina and thorough attention to her pleasure, Allison had dozed for a few minutes, then allowed him to scoop her up and tuck her into bed. She hadn't expected her tough and sexy best friend to be so tenderhearted.

But something had roused her. She reached for Logan and discovered he was awake as well.

Under the covers he pressed his cell phone into her palm. "Stay here," he said at her ear. A moment later, he left the bed without making a sound and she scooted under the covers, reading the string of text messages.

Jenna had found Tanner through the GPS on his car and notified both Logan and Hank of his direction as he'd driven through town to the marina near his home. The car had remained there, but they suspected he was in his boat. Hank had moved toward the dock near her complex to provide backup to Logan.

The last message was a grainy, still picture of Tanner in the condo's riverfront courtyard. He must have come up the river to the private dock, confident he could get to her. The bastard.

She started to jump out of bed to help, but Logan was back and he kept her still with a heavy hand on her hip. "Get to the bathroom and call 9-1-1. Stay on the call no matter what you hear."

She could do so much more than call for help. And knowing her, he had to understand that she didn't want her nasty ex to hurt her best friend, now lover. Her immediate protest was cut short by a sound on the other side of the bedroom door.

"Go." Logan moved away, the moonlight through the glass highlighting the hard planes of his naked body.

She took his phone and tiptoed to the bathroom to make the call. A rush of cool and humid air washed over her. Logan had gone out to the balcony through the bedroom door. Goosebumps chased over her skin. She grabbed her tank top and shorts from the laundry hamper and pulled them back on. Logan would sneak up on Tanner, take him by surprise and it would be over.

As quietly as possible, she reported the break in and her address to the emergency operator.

She even named Tanner Aultman as the likely intruder.

She behaved and played her part, right up until the gunshot cracked through the darkness. Dropping the cell phone, she ran to the balcony, taking Logan's route to stay out of the way, but she had to be sure Logan was all right.

She tiptoed across the cool concrete and peered through the glass doors of the living room. Logan and Tanner were grappling, her front door was ajar, and the gun had landed on the floor not far from the bedroom door.

She scurried back through the bedroom, cringing at every grunt and curse of the fight and the crash that probably indicated the painful demise of her furniture.

As long as Logan survived.

She eased open the bedroom door and inched her way down the hall to the gun. It was hard to see through the shadows, but turning on a light could distract Logan. Her fingers touched the gun and she pulled it close, scooting back out of sight.

Why didn't she hear any sirens? And where was Hank?

Another crash quickly followed by cursing. It was

up to her. She could do this. She could aim a weapon at another person—at Tanner—and call intermission on this fight until the police arrived.

With her courage screwed down tight, she stood up, holding the gun as she'd been taught during a class she'd taken a few years back with some girlfriends.

"Stop!" she shouted. But she was too late. She watched, horrified as the men went through the glass door. Logan had leaped into this fight without a stitch of clothing. To protect her.

She kept the gun aimed at the floor as she followed them. Tanner was under Logan, bucking and swinging his fists, to no avail. Logan drove a knee hard into the man's side, but when he pulled back for another strike, Tanner rallied, twisting away and gaining his feet.

Streaks of blood marred the balcony. Logan didn't need to take any more wounds on her behalf.

"Stop!" she shouted again. "I *will* shoot you, Tanner."

"You wouldn't dare," he snarled.

"My house. Castle law," she snapped.

Logan glanced her way as he gained his feet and Tanner jumped on the advantage, grabbing Logan and bending him back over the railing, an arm to his throat.

Worth the risk, she decided. Easy enough to spot a good target, even in the dark, when one man was clothed and the other buck naked. She pulled the trigger, satisfied when Tanner reared back and grabbed his butt, a string of curses spewing into the night.

Logan shoved him onto the chaise. "Don't move." Then he walked up and took the gun from Allison's limp hand, holding it on Tanner. "Nice shot, sweetheart."

"You're welcome," she replied, burying her face in his chest.

"Make a move, Tanner, and I'll shoot you in the gut," Logan vowed. "It's a mess to heal."

Tanner only glared at him.

"Did you call the cops?" he asked Allison.

She eased back just far enough to turn on the outside lights. Her stomach twisted at the streaks of blood that seemed to be everywhere. "The emergency operator is probably still on the phone."

"And where is the phone?"

"Bedroom floor. I'll get it and some shorts for you."

"Appreciate that."

She made it a quick trip to the bedroom and back, taking over the gun while Logan pulled on a pair of cargo shorts. The emergency operator was still on the line and Allison gave her an update, including who was armed and who was injured.

He reclaimed the weapon, keeping it trained on Tanner, and she held onto the phone while she retrieved the first aid kit from the kitchen. The police arrived before she could start cleaning Logan's wounds and Hank Patterson was right behind them with the paramedics on his heels.

Her home was suddenly bursting at the seams with voices and questions and more information than she could process. She wanted Logan and peace and quiet. But that wasn't happening. At least Tanner had been taken into custody and escorted to the ambulance.

Apparently the intrusion and the entire fight had moved much faster in real time than it had seemed to her.

Hank hadn't followed Tanner upstairs because he'd been checking out the boat. "I took photos," he said, handing his cell phone to the responding police officer who had taken charge of the scene. "I don't know about you, but those aren't the tools I use on a fishing trip."

Officer Davis carried himself like a cop with years of experience. She'd noticed deep lines framing his dark brown eyes and a little gray in his

LOGAN

neatly trimmed beard. Looking at the images on Hank's phone, he blanched. "Not even close."

"Do I want to know?" Allison asked Logan under her breath.

He shook his head. "Whatever it is, Aultman didn't have anything pleasant in mind."

She could accept that.

Logan refused to go to the hospital for treatment, letting Allison and the second team of paramedics wash and treat his wounds.

"You'll want to stay off your feet as much as possible for a few days," the paramedic instructed as he packed up his kit.

Hank snorted. "We'll make sure he does."

At last it was just the three of them and she went for the broom to start cleaning up the biggest messes. "Let me," Hank said. "You've been through enough."

"No. I, um, need to do something."

Hank and Logan exchanged a look. "Why don't you pack up whatever you need for the next few days? Jenna called in a cleaning service. I'll wait here for them."

It dawned on her she'd have to deal with the owner's association and the insurance claim and the details snowballed until she couldn't take anymore. Tears, hot and unwelcome, streamed down her face

165

and embarrassment leaped onto the pile of emotions vying for control.

She vaguely registered the movement as Logan pried the broom from her hands. He scooped her up and carried her back to the bedroom. "T-this isn't staying off your feet," she scolded. "Give me a minute. I'm sorry I'm such a mess."

"You're no mess, you're my hero," he said.

She choked on the compliment. "You're hurt because of me. Again."

"Not hurt. I'll give you annoyed and mildly sore."

She rolled her eyes and he chuckled. "Look at that, you've stopped crying."

He brushed his thumbs over her damp cheeks and then kissed her with a tenderness that soothed her down to her bones.

"I'm hurt because of a selfish asshole. *You* had nothing to do with it."

"Fine. You should still get off your feet."

He grinned. "Sweetheart, I plan to do just that as soon as we're out of here. I'll even let you drive to the resort."

"The Ellington?"

"Yes." He grinned from ear to ear. "Jenna arranged everything for us and Hank meant what he said about waiting for the cleaning crew."

"We're having brunch there on Sunday. With the Pattersons."

"I'm aware. Now we'll only have to walk." He bent his head and kissed her, spinning her up for much better reasons. Easing back, he smiled. "Let's pack."

CHAPTER 14

ONCE THEY REACHED the suite at the resort, they fell into bed and didn't wake until after noon. Thanks to Jenna they were pampered at the spa with massages and a facial for Allison. Logan received updates on Tanner, but he didn't share them right away, wanting her to get some rest and distance from the entire mess.

As the sun set, he found Allison lounging on the balcony. She wore a dark purple bikini with white flowers and held a glass of whiskey in one hand, her gaze on the water. To look at her, it was impossible to know she'd been through any kind of ordeal.

"How are you feeling?" He wanted to touch her but he was a little afraid. Many times people were sensitive about contact after an attack and she'd been through so much in the past days.

"Is there a reason you're treating me like glass? I've been a mess lately, but I'm not fragile."

No, she was brave as hell *and* the most precious thing in the world. If she was ever hurt, truly wounded or—God, forbid—taken from him, he would be the one shattered.

"Sweetheart, I'm sorry you've been subjected to all of this. I wish I could've stopped him sooner."

"You've been distant all day. If something's changed, just tell me."

"I've been trying to give you space."

She gave a little snort that might have been a laugh under better circumstances and swung her feet over the edge of the chaise until her knees were bumping his. "I actually want you to hold me."

"I can do that." Setting their drinks aside, he pulled her into his lap and cuddled her close. Her body relaxed against him and the uncertainty that had been knotting his stomach melted away. This was exactly where he belonged.

"I don't understand how Tanner thought he could win," she murmured.

"He's twisted. And desperate. Jenna discovered he's on the verge of bankruptcy and the money he's been flashing around isn't his."

"How did I not know that?" she mused.

"He didn't want you to know that. He didn't want

anyone to know how close he was to losing at all," Logan replied. "Officer Davis left a message that Tanner is talking as fast as he can, making deals to save his skin. Even if his shady partners don't find him, he'll never trouble you again."

"So what now? What about us?" she asked, her voice barely more than a whisper.

He wanted it all, with her. "You make me feel like I can be home, Allison. Home and whole. I know this is new for us, but I'm all in. I'm yours for as long as you'll have me." He touched his nose to hers. "I love you."

"Logan." She pushed her hands through his hair, as she kissed him, long and deep.

She hadn't given him the words back, but it didn't matter. He could wait. He'd never tire of her touch. And he would miss it like hell when she finally told him to leave.

"What do you want, Allison? Ask me for anything and I'll see that you have it."

Her smile lit a thousand wishes in his heart. "I want you, Logan. I love you too."

"I...what?" He couldn't quite wrap his head around it.

"You heard me," she teased.

"Say it again."

She grinned. "I love you, Logan." She took his face between her hands and kissed him soundly. "I can't really remember a day that I haven't loved you. But this is more now. It's not just because you're my best friend or because you saved my life. I love you for all that you are outside of those marvelous factors."

His arms banded around her. He would give her anything, do anything to make her happy. It was more than he ever expected. "I love you, Allison. It started way back when we were kids and it's grown into something I didn't know to wish for." He smoothed her hair back from her face. "Wherever life takes us, I don't want to go through it with anyone but you."

"You mean it." She sounded as breathless as he felt.

"I've never lied to you. Never will. I can't promise you yachts or annual vacations in the Maldives."

"You know I don't need any of those promises," she said.

"I also can't promise you every day will be a picnic."

She kissed him again. "Then we'll just enjoy those picnic days all the more."

More content than he ever thought he'd be, they

snuggled together, watching the brilliant colors of the sunset paint the sky, lost in each other and found in love.

The End

Off The Radar

For full details on all of Regan's books visit ReganBlack.com and

enjoy excerpts from each of her sexy, adrenaline-fueled novels.

Black Ice, Book 4 in Stormwatch, a multi-author series

what she knew, Book 4 in Breakdown, a multi-author series

Knight Traveler Series

The Matchmaker Series

Escape Club Heroes, Harlequin Romantic Suspense

The Riley Code, Harlequin Romantic Suspense

Colton Family saga, a multi-author series, Harlequin Romantic Suspense

ABOUT REGAN BLACK

Regan Black, a USA Today and internationally best-selling author, writes award-winning, action-packed romances featuring kick-butt heroines and the sexy heroes who fall in love with them. Raised in the Midwest and California, she and her husband share their empty nest with two adorably arrogant cats in the South Carolina Lowcountry where the rich blend of legend, romance, and history fuels her imagination.

For early access to new book releases, exclusive prizes, and much more, subscribe to the monthly newsletter at ReganBlack.com/perks.

Keep up with Regan online:
www.ReganBlack.com
Facebook
Twitter
Instagram
Or follow Regan at:
BookBub
Amazon

facebook.com/ReganBlack.fans
twitter.com/ReganBlack
instagram.com/reganblackauthor

BROTHERHOOD PROTECTORS

ORIGINAL SERIES BY ELLE JAMES

Hot SEAL Bachelor Party (SEALs in Paradise)

ABOUT ELLE JAMES

ELLE JAMES also writing as MYLA JACKSON is a *New York Times* and *USA Today* Bestselling author of books including cowboys, intrigues and paranormal adventures that keep her readers on the edges of their seats. With over eighty works in a variety of sub-genres and lengths she has published with Harlequin, Samhain, Ellora's Cave, Kensington, Cleis Press, and Avon. When she's not at her computer, she's traveling, snow skiing, boating, or riding her ATV, dreaming up new stories. Learn more about Elle James at www.ellejames.com

Website | Facebook | Twitter | GoodReads | Newsletter | BookBub | Amazon

Follow Elle!
www.ellejames.com
ellejames@ellejames.com

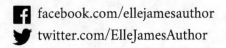

facebook.com/ellejamesauthor
twitter.com/ElleJamesAuthor

Printed in the USA
CPSIA information can be obtained
at www.ICGtesting.com
LVHW021555101224
798795LV00010B/505

* 9 7 8 1 6 2 6 9 5 3 3 5 2 *